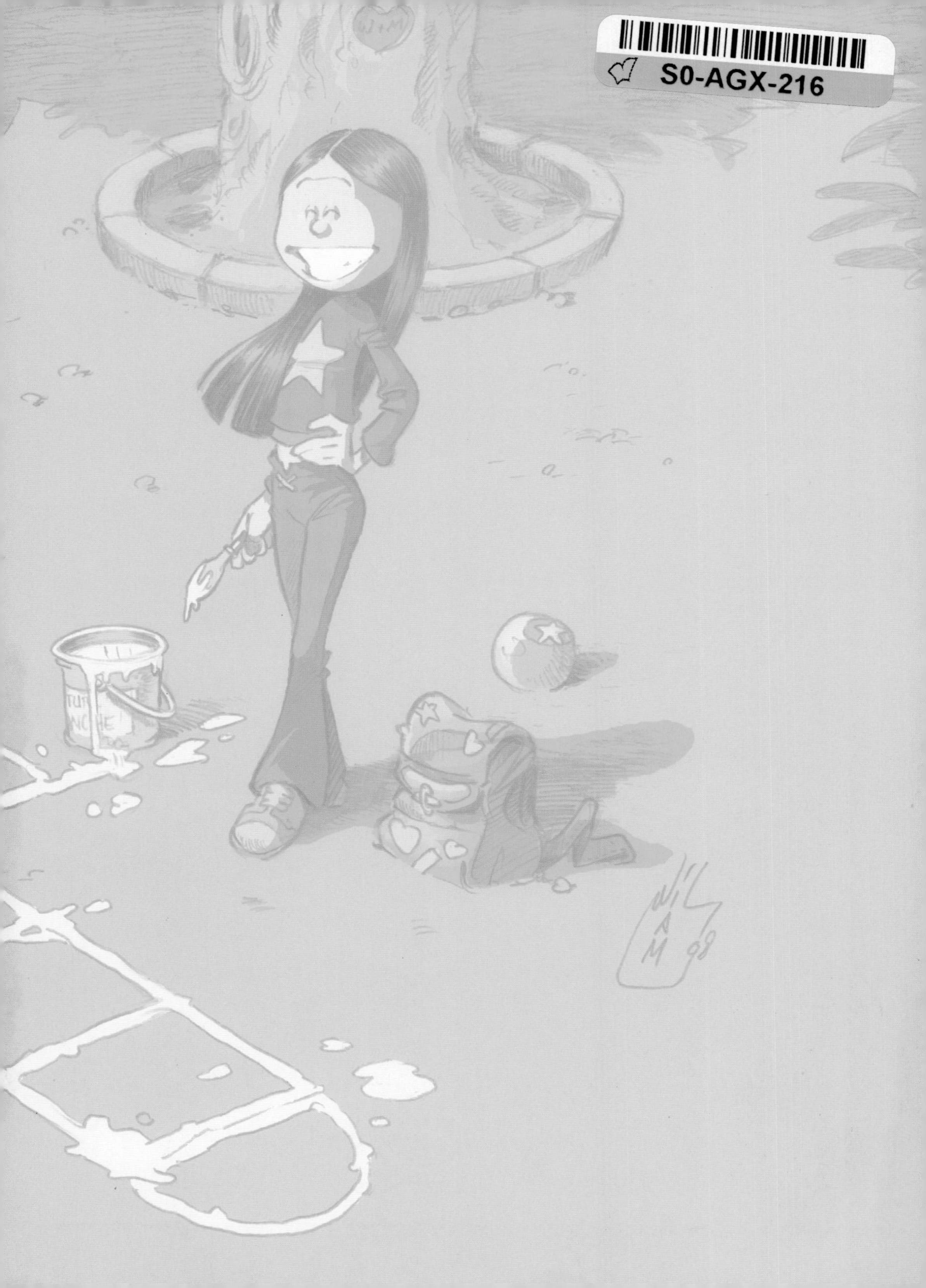

Art and colors
William

Story
Cazenove & William

PAPERCUTZ

Les Sisters by Cazenove and William
© 2008–2010 Bamboo Édition
Sisters, characters and related indicia are copyright, trademark and exclusive license of Bamboo Edition.
All other editorial material © 2016 by Papercutz
All rights reserved.

The Sisters
#1 "Just Like Family"
Story by Cazenove and William
Art and color by William
Cover by William
Translation by Nanette McGuinness and Anne & Owen Smith
Lettering by Wilson Ramos, Jr. and Dawn Guzzo

"A Style of Our Own"
Story by Cazenove and William
Art and color by William
Translation by Anne & Owen Smith
Lettering by Grace Lu
© 2016 for this Work in English language by Papercutz.

Papercutz books may be purchased for business or promotional use. For information on bulk purchases please contact Macmillan Corporate and Premium Sales Department at
(800) 221-7945 x5442.

Production – Dawn Guzzo
Production Coordinator – Jeff Whitman
Editor – Carol M. Burrell
Associate Editor – Bethany Bryan
Jim Salicrup
Editor-in-Chief

PB ISBN: 978-1-62991-493-0
HC ISBN: 978-1-62991-470-1

Printed in China
November 2016 by O.G. Printing Productions, LTD.

Distributed by Macmillan
Second Papercutz Printing

To my two beloved tornadoes: Wendy and Marine. And to Sandrine, their mom.

Thank you, "gag brain" Christophe, for your help and brilliance. Thank you, Olivier, for your confidence.

I also dedicate this volume to Franck Tourneret and to the members of the great "Baywin" forum, where this project, in part, first came to life.

Thank you, Anelor, for your small suggestions about slang and your critical eye. Thank you, reader who holds this volume in your hands: may you have as much fun reading it as I had creating it.

—William

1: Just Like Family

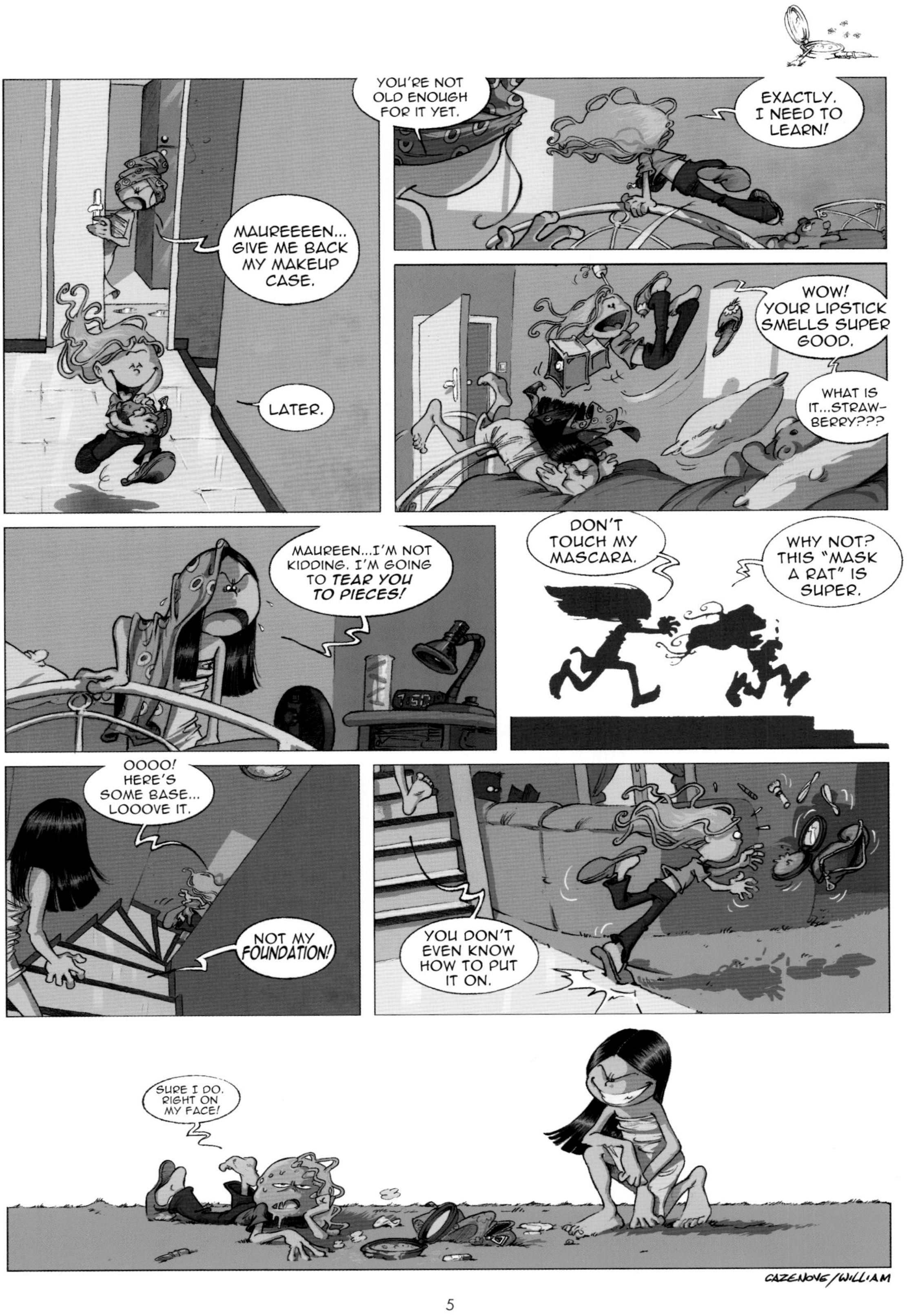
MAUREEEEN... GIVE ME BACK MY MAKEUP CASE.
LATER.
YOU'RE NOT OLD ENOUGH FOR IT YET.
EXACTLY. I NEED TO LEARN!
WOW! YOUR LIPSTICK SMELLS SUPER GOOD.
WHAT IS IT...STRAWBERRY???
MAUREEN...I'M NOT KIDDING. I'M GOING TO TEAR YOU TO PIECES!
DON'T TOUCH MY MASCARA.
WHY NOT? THIS "MASK A RAT" IS SUPER.
OOOO! HERE'S SOME BASE... LOOOVE IT.
NOT MY FOUNDATION!
YOU DON'T EVEN KNOW HOW TO PUT IT ON.
SURE I DO. RIGHT ON MY FACE!
CAZENOVE/WILLIAM

IT'S SO FRUSTRATING. I WISH I HAD CURLS INSTEAD OF *STRAIGHT* HAIR!

IF ONLY I WERE A *BLOOONDE...*

AND ME A *BRUNETTE...*

AND I HAVE *CURLY* HAIR BUT I WISH IT WAS *STRAAAIGHT.*

WAAAAHH

PLUS MAUREEN IS A LOUSY FIRST NAME. I'D RATHER BE A WENDYYY.

AND ME A MAUREEEEN.

THAT'S ENOUGH! YOU'RE NEVER HAPPY! GO TO YOUR ROOMS THIS INSTANT!

?!

HER ROOM IS BETTER THAN MI-I-INE!

CAZENOVE/WILLIAM

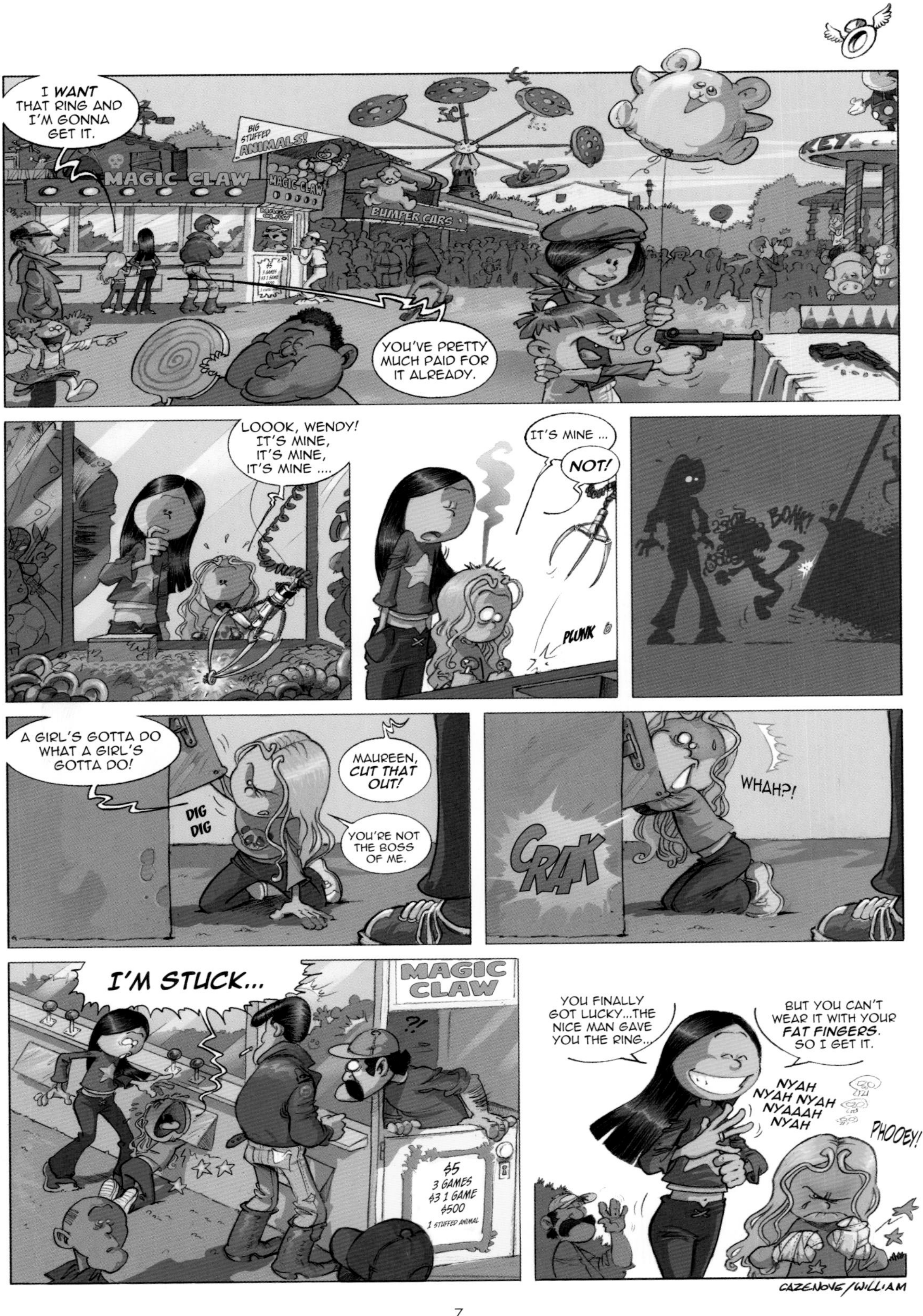

I WANT THAT RING AND I'M GONNA GET IT.
YOU'VE PRETTY MUCH PAID FOR IT ALREADY.
MAGIC CLAW
BIG STUFFED ANIMALS!
BUMPER CARS
LOOOK, WENDY! IT'S MINE, IT'S MINE, IT'S MINE ....
IT'S MINE ...
NOT!
PLUNK
BONK!
A GIRL'S GOTTA DO WHAT A GIRL'S GOTTA DO!
DIG DIG
MAUREEN, CUT THAT OUT!
YOU'RE NOT THE BOSS OF ME.
CRAK
WHAH?!
I'M STUCK...
MAGIC CLAW
?!
$5 3 GAMES $3 1 GAME $500 1 STUFFED ANIMAL
YOU FINALLY GOT LUCKY...THE NICE MAN GAVE YOU THE RING...
BUT YOU CAN'T WEAR IT WITH YOUR FAT FINGERS. SO I GET IT.
NYAH NYAH NYAH NYAAAH NYAH
PHOOEY!
CAZENOVE/WILLIAM

PHEW, I'M WIPED OUT!

THERE YOU GO! ARE YOU ALL SETTLED IN, BUN BUN?

ARE YOU FEELING LONELY?! DO YOU WANT SOME COMPANY?!

HE'S SO CUTE!

ALL RIGHT, CUDDLES AND PUDGE, COME JOIN US.

WHY NOT RAVIOLI AND THE WHOLE GANG, TOO?

I FALL FOR IT EVERY TIME. WHAT A LAMEBRAIN!

CAZENOVE/WILLIAM

YOU'RE THE BEST DADDY EVER!

YESSSS?

CAN I GET A DOG?

PRETTY PLS. PRETTY PLS. PRETTY PLS. PRETTY PLS.

A DOG IS A LOT OF WORK, WENDY. YOU HAVE TO TAKE IT FOR WALKS...

YOU HAVE TO BRUSH IT...

A...A...A...

A..CHOo!

...PLAY WITH IT...

HEY! THAT'S MY DIARY!

FEED IT EVERY DAY...

HEY! THAT'S *MY* BREAKFAST. LET GO!

GRRR!!

OKAY! ENOUGH ALREADY!

I CHANGED MY MIND!

I ALREADY DO ALL THAT FOR MY *SISTER!*

WENDYYYYY...

DO MY HAIR!

CAZENOVE/WILL·AM

??? ???

I THINK IT'S A POT OF *WAX.*

PEEYEW! THAT STINKS TO HIGH HEAVEN! I'LL *NEVER* EAT THAT!

LOL. IT'S NOT FOR EATING, SILLY. IT'S FOR REMOVING *HAIR.*

HAIR ?

YOU'RE SUCH A LAMEBRAIN.

MOM USES IT TO REMOVE HER MOUSTACHE.

MOM DOESN'T HAVE A *MOUSTACHE!*

AND SHE DOESN'T HAVE HAIR ON HER LEGS!

OF COURSE NOT, BECAUSE SHE USES *WAX!*

IT'S FOR HER LEGS, TOO.

HUMPH!

MFFFF

HEY, LADY, YOU COULD USE A WHOLE POT OF WAX, PRONTO!

CAZENOVE/WILLIAM

WENDYYYY

I HAD A *HORRIBLE* NIGHTMARE. CAN I COME IN WITH YOU?

WHAH?

UMM, SURE. WHAT ELSE IS A *BIG SISTER* FOR?!

COME ON, GET IN. TELL ME ALL ABOUT IT.

I DREAMED THAT WHEN I WOKE UP, I COULDN'T GET MY SLIPPERS ON...

BUT MY FEET WERE *HUMONGOUS*.

THAT'S NOT SO BAD!

THERE, THERE. YOUR FEET ARE BACK TO NORMAL.

SNIFF

BUT *EVERYTHING* WAS TOO SMALL. MY SOCKS, PANTS, UNDIES, SWEATERS...

IT STILL DOESN'T SOUND LIKE A NIGHTMARE.

I WAS HUGE BECAUSE I REALIZED I'D BECOME *YOU!*

IMAGINE THE TRAUMA!

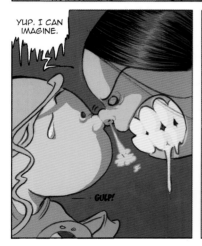

YUP. I CAN IMAGINE.

GULP!

SLAM!

HEY! IS *THAT* WHAT A BIG SISTER'S FOR?

CAZENOVE/WILLIAM

I LOVE HIP-HOP!

Dance Classes
Hip-Hop
Classical
Ballroom
Tango
Waltz
Bourrée
Rain

YEAH, IT'S MEGA FUN!

IT'S TOTALLY TRENDY.

IT'S SO WICKED.

IT ROCKS.

IT'S ULTRA COOL.

THE TIP OF THE TOP. IT'S HIP. IT'S HOP.

SLIIIIIIIDE

IT'S SUPER-AWESOME.

WHEEE! IT'S GOT A GOOD VIBE.

HIP-HOP IS...

HIP-HOP IS SO FIVE MINUTES AGO.

FOR SURE.

HIC! HOP! HIP! HOPS!

CAZENOVE/WILLIAM

TODAY, MOM GAVE US A SPECIAL PRESENT...

COOL! AND IT'S EXACTLY MY SIZE!

WOW!

HEE HEE

...SUPERHERO COSTUMES.

I'M *W.*

TREMBLE IN FEAR! *M* IS HERE.

NOW WE CAN SAVE THE WORLD, LIKE IN A *VIDEO GAME!*

ZAP DEMONS, LIKE *ON TV!*

SHAAZAM!

COWABUNGA!

NOOOO... NOT *W* AND *M!*

FIGHT MAD SCIENTISTS AND PROTECT THE PLANET, LIKE IN THE MOVIES.

TODAY, DADDY GAVE US A PRESENT, TOO...

WENDY, MAUREEN...

...OUR FIRST MISSION.

HMPH...

PFFT...

CAZENOVE/WILL:AM

3 A.M. ...GET UP...

BRUSH BRUSH

PSSH

LA LA LA LA LA LA LA LA

WHADDA YOU DOIN' UP AT THIS HOUR???

YAWN.

WHAT IF PAPARAZZI SHOW UP WHEN I'M SLEEPING?

IT COULD HAPPEN.

CAZENOVE/WILLIAM

GONE?!

COOL!

COAST IS CLEAR.

HELLO, WENDY'S SECRET DIARY...

I'VE DREAMED ABOUT GETTING MY HANDS ON YOU FOR AGES.

THINK OF ITS PRACTICAL VALUE. IF I DON'T KNOW WHO SHE HAS A CRUSH ON, HOW CAN I BUG HER ABOUT HIM?!

HOW DOES THIS THING OPEN?

OOPS! WHAT A CRUMMY PADLOCK!

COAC!

ZIP!

BIG MISTAKE!

IF WENDY FINDS OUT SHE'LL SKIN ME ALIVE.

FIXED IT! SHE'LL NEVER NOTICE.

I'M SO GOOD!

BAM!

MAUREEEEEEN

WOW... SHE MUST HAVE A SIXTH SENSE!

CAZENOVE/WILLIAM

15

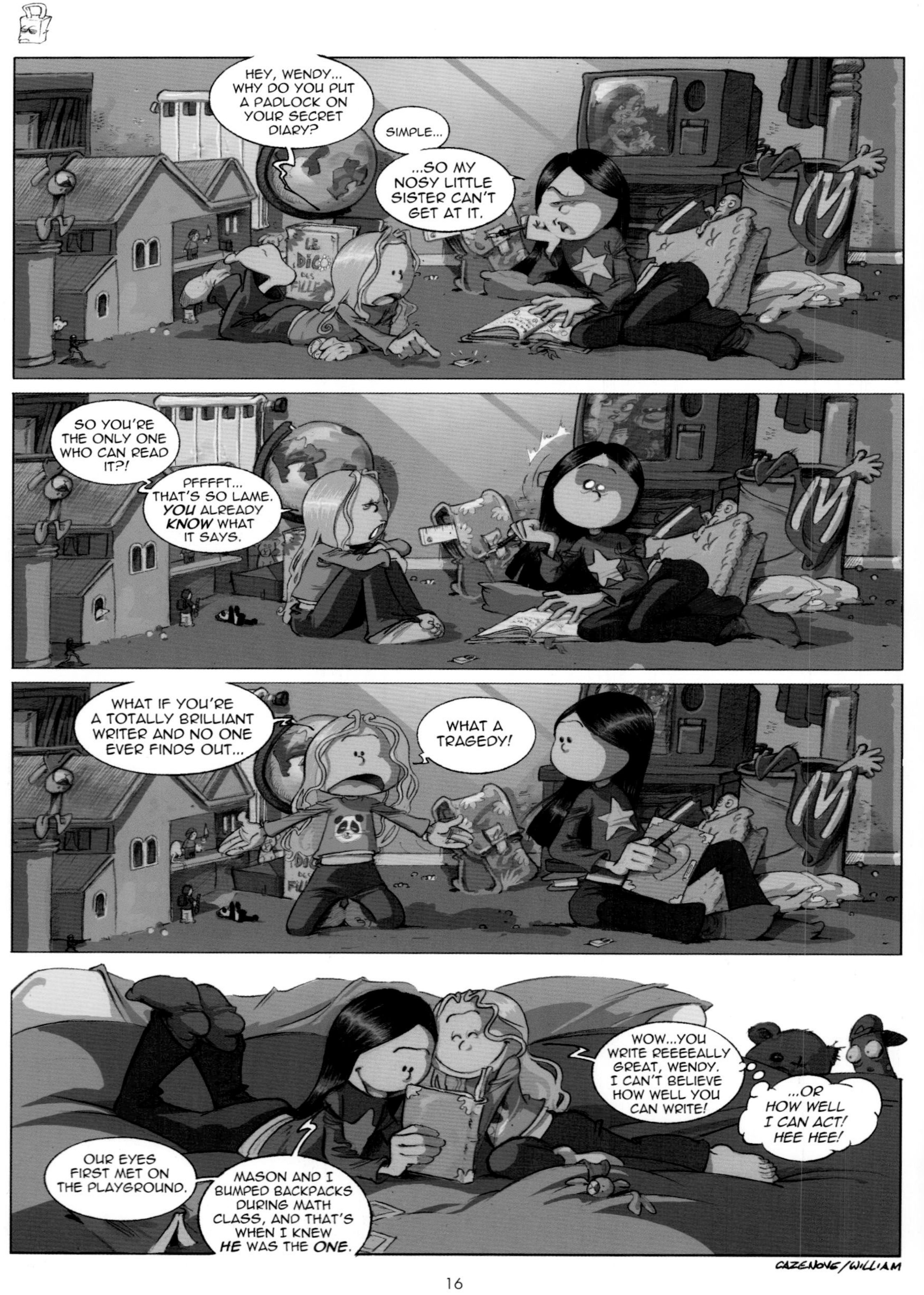
HEY, WENDY... WHY DO YOU PUT A PADLOCK ON YOUR SECRET DIARY?
SIMPLE...
...SO MY NOSY LITTLE SISTER CAN'T GET AT IT.
LE DICO DES FILLES
SO YOU'RE THE ONLY ONE WHO CAN READ IT?!
PFFFFT... THAT'S SO LAME. YOU ALREADY KNOW WHAT IT SAYS.
WHAT IF YOU'RE A TOTALLY BRILLIANT WRITER AND NO ONE EVER FINDS OUT...
WHAT A TRAGEDY!
WOW...YOU WRITE REEEEALLY GREAT, WENDY. I CAN'T BELIEVE HOW WELL YOU CAN WRITE!
...OR HOW WELL I CAN ACT! HEE HEE!
OUR EYES FIRST MET ON THE PLAYGROUND.
MASON AND I BUMPED BACKPACKS DURING MATH CLASS, AND THAT'S WHEN I KNEW HE WAS THE ONE.
CAZENOVE/WILLIAM

?!

YUUUUCK! WHAT'RE YOU DOING?

WHASH YOU MEAN?

ARE YOU STILL SUCKING YOUR THUMB?!

IF YOU KEEP THAT UP, IT'LL TURN BLACK AND FALL OFF.

WAAAAAAH

SHHHHHH... STOP HOWLING. YOU'LL WAKE UP MOM AND DAD!

LOOK, FORGET WHAT I SAID AND GO TO SLEEP.

I CAN'T NOW, I'M SURE I CAN'T!

ARRGH! STOP WORRYING ABOUT IT!

BUT, BUT... B-B-B...

OKAY, OKAY. WE'LL FIGURE SOMETHING OUT!

SNUFFLE.

CHCK CHCK CHCK

Z Z Z

CAZENOVE/WILLIAM

17

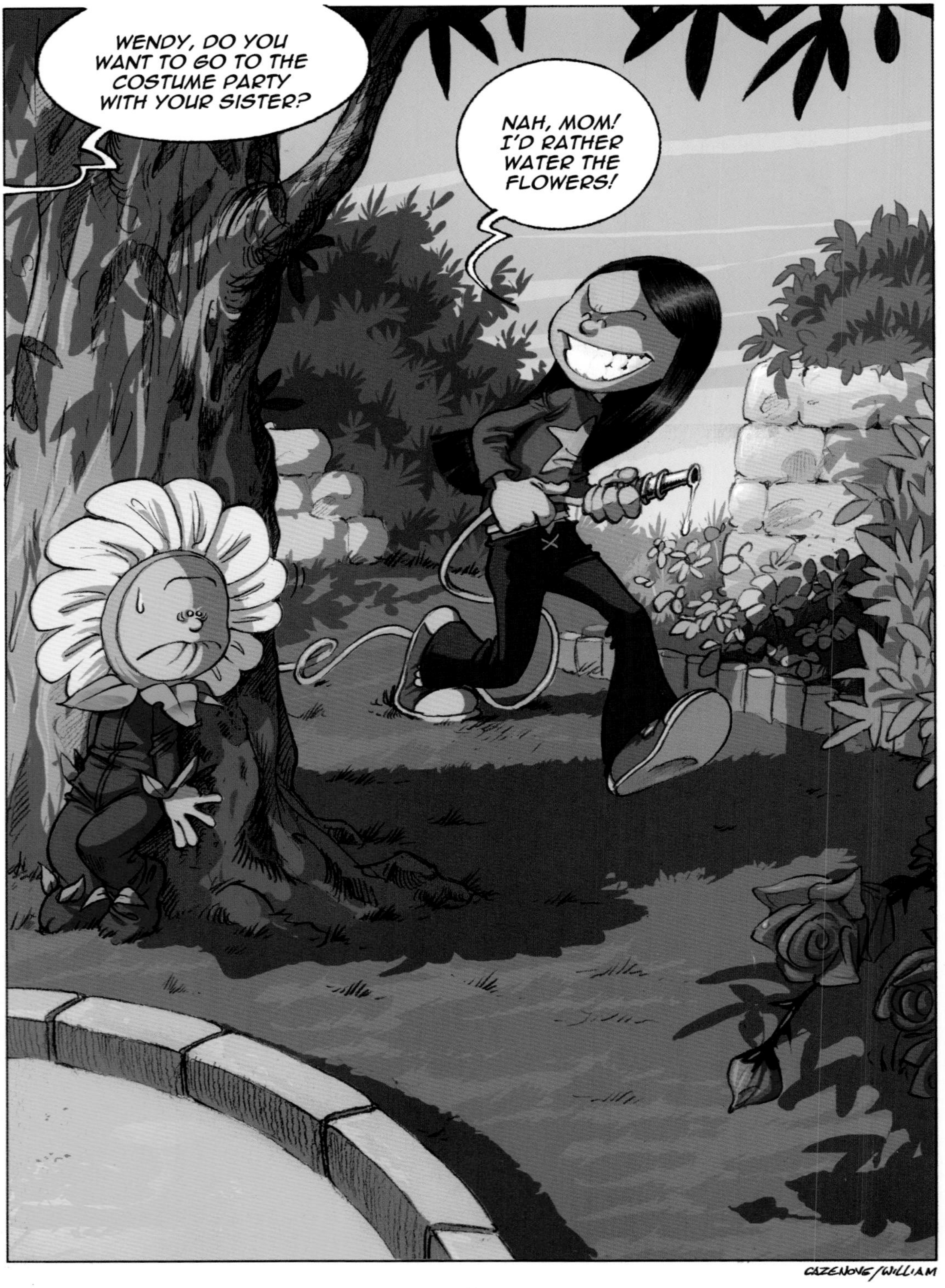
WENDY, DO YOU WANT TO GO TO THE COSTUME PARTY WITH YOUR SISTER?
NAH, MOM! I'D RATHER WATER THE FLOWERS!
CAZENOVE/WILLIAM

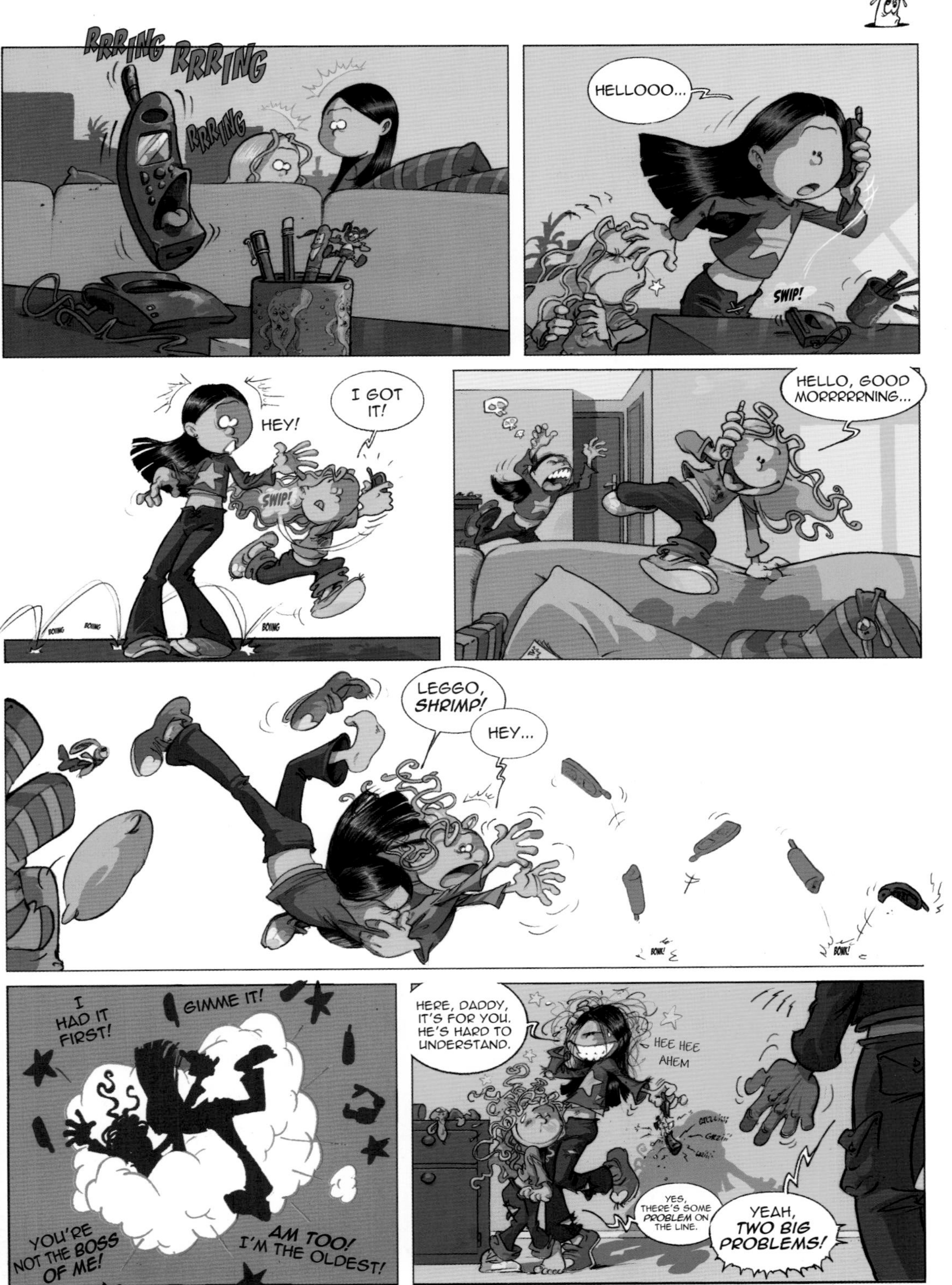
RRRING RRRING
RRRING
HELLOOO...
SWIP!
HEY!
I GOT IT!
SWIP!
BOING BOING BOING
HELLO, GOOD MORRRRRNING...
LEGGO, SHRIMP!
HEY...
BONK!
BONK!
I HAD IT FIRST!
GIMME IT!
YOU'RE NOT THE BOSS OF ME!
AM TOO! I'M THE OLDEST!
HERE, DADDY, IT'S FOR YOU. HE'S HARD TO UNDERSTAND.
HEE HEE AHEM
YES, THERE'S SOME PROBLEM ON THE LINE.
YEAH, TWO BIG PROBLEMS!
CAZENOVE/WILLIAM

THE DIVA WITH 100 PLATINUM RECORDS IS IN DA HOUSE.

LOL. SHE'S SUCH A SHOW OFF!

CLIK!

CLIK!

THE **STAR** POSE.

THE **STATUE** POSE.

THE **PIN-UP** POSE.

THE **DANCER** POSE.

CLIK!

CLIK!

CLIK!

UH-OH!

THE **CAST** POSE.

ORTHO PEDICS

CAZENOVE/WILLIAM

20

I CAN'T BELIEVE IT! NO MATTER WHAT I SAY...

...MY PARENTS WON'T GET ME A CELL PHONE.

ME NEITHER...

EVEN IF I SWEAR IT'S ONLY FOR EMERGENCIES.

THEY WON'T BUDGE!

SAME HERE!

WITH MY ALLOWANCE, IT'LL TAKE 12-1/2 YEARS TO SAVE UP FOR ONE!

BY THEN, CELL PHONES WILL BE OUT OF STYLE!

TOTALLY!

I DUNNO IF YOU'VE NOTICED, BUT THE SISTERS HAVE ONE.

REALLY?

NO KIDDING?

YEAH, BUT THEIR PARENTS FOUND A WAY TO KEEP THEIR USAGE DOWN...

THEY GAVE THE PHONE TO WENDY AND THE BATTERY TO MAUREEN.

LOL

LOL   ROFL

GIMME THAT, SHRIMP!

IN YOUR DREAMS. IT'S MY TURN NOW!

CAZENOVE/WILLIAM

NO, NO, NO, MOM AND DAD. THIS EVENING *WE'LL* TAKE CARE OF *EVERYTHING*, JUST LIKE GROWNUPS!

LOOK, WENDY. I FOUND THEIR WEDDING CHINA.

CLAP!

YUCCK!

HOLY COW! EVEN THE DUST IS VINTAGE!

THEY DESERVE THE PRETTIEST GLASSES.

YEAH...THE ONES WITH CALVIN AND HOBBES!

LOOK WHAT I CAN DO WITH NAPKINS!

SALT, PEPPER, KNIVES, FORKS...

YIKES! WE ALMOST FORGOT THE CANDLES.

GOOD CATCH!

LADIES AND GENTLEMEN, YOU MAY COME IN!

TADAAAA!

WOW! BEAUTIFUL TABLE, GIRLS!

WHAT'S ON THE MENU?

...

IT'S NOT OUR FAULT! WE'RE JUST KIDS!

YEAH, WE CAN'T THINK OF *EVERYTHING*.

CAZENOVE/WILLIAM

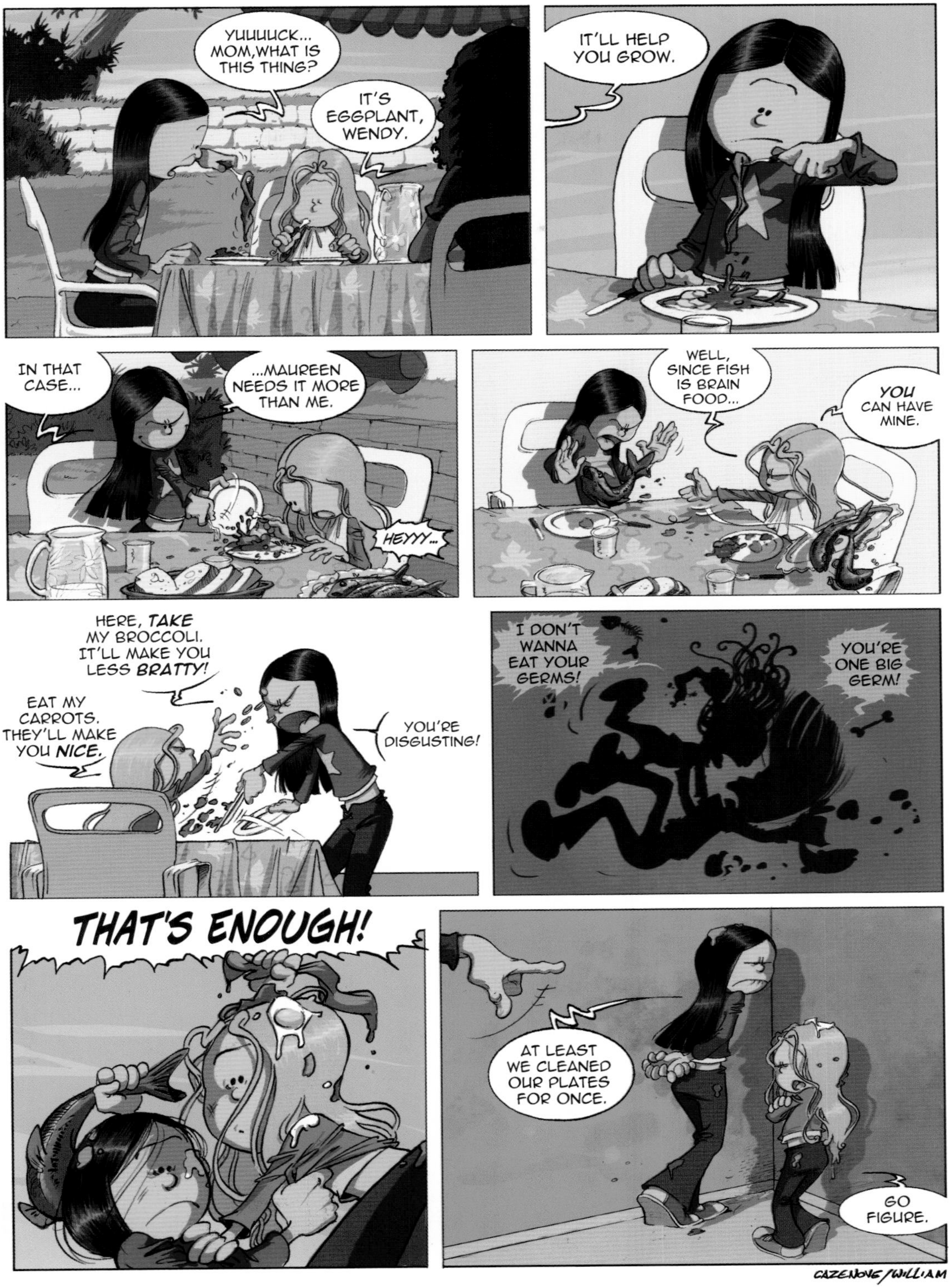

YUUUUCK... MOM, WHAT IS THIS THING?
IT'S EGGPLANT, WENDY.
IT'LL HELP YOU GROW.
IN THAT CASE...
...MAUREEN NEEDS IT MORE THAN ME.
HEYYY...
WELL, SINCE FISH IS BRAIN FOOD...
YOU CAN HAVE MINE.
HERE, TAKE MY BROCCOLI. IT'LL MAKE YOU LESS BRATTY!
EAT MY CARROTS. THEY'LL MAKE YOU NICE.
YOU'RE DISGUSTING!
I DON'T WANNA EAT YOUR GERMS!
YOU'RE ONE BIG GERM!
THAT'S ENOUGH!
AT LEAST WE CLEANED OUR PLATES FOR ONCE.
GO FIGURE.
CAZENOVE/WILLIAM

CUT IT OUT!

I CAN'T STAND IT ANYMORE!

YOU CAN'T PLAY *HEAVY METAL* ON A FLUTE...

IT'S LAME.

HOW'S IT LAME?

YOU JUST DON'T LIKE *HEAVY METAL.*

AND *YOU* HAVE *NO* MUSICAL TALENT.

STAY CALM... ZEN...DON'T RIP HER TO SHREDS. ZEN ZEN ZEN ZEN

YOU CAN'T PLAY *METAL*...

...ON A *WOODEN* INSTRUMENT!

REALLY?

SNIP

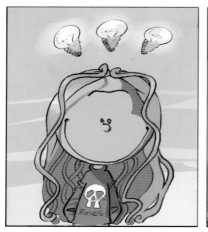

BAM!

BAM! BAM!

YOU'RE RIGHT! IT SOUNDS WAY BETTER WITH *REAL METAL!*

BOOHOO HOO HOO

CAZENOVE/WILLIAM

WOOOW, MAUREEN. YOUR PERFUME SMELLS GREAT!

WHERE'D YOU GET IT?

IS IT YOUR MOM'S?

WHAT BRAND IS IT?

IT'S VERY FRUITY. WHAT'S IT CALLED?

MMMMMM. I'M SERIOUSLY JEALOUS.

HEE HEE HEE

SNIFF

SNIFF

ALL I SMELL IS APPLE.

HUH.

HMPH! WE WEREN'T TALKING TO YOU.

GRRRR

YOU'RE SUCH A BOY! LEAVE US ALONE.

BLAH BLAH BLAH

HE'S RIGHT, IT DOES SMELL LIKE APPLE.

MMMMM. AND CITRUS.

TELL US. WHAT IS IT?

IF YOU'RE NICE TO ME, I'LL TELL YOU... SOME DAY.

I'LL DO YOUR HOMEWORK.

I'LL CARRY YOUR BACKPACK.

MAUREEN, IT'S SWEET OF YOU TO HELP WITH THE DISHES EVERY MORNING...

...BUT IF YOU USE SO MUCH DISHWASHING LIQUID...

...YOU'LL SMELL LIKE IT ALL DAY.

FRUITY
DISHWASHING LIQUID

CAZENOVE/WILLIAM

25

THE MAAAAIL'S HEEERE!

ELECTRIC BILL, PHONE BILL, INSURANCE, MORTGAGE, WATER...

PHOOEY...

PHOOEY...

WHAT'VE YOU GOT?

TA...XES... FI...NAL... RE...MIIIN... DER

WAIT, LOOK. THERE'S STILL STUFF IN THERE.

OH, YEAH. WAY IN THE BACK.

THEY FINALLY CAME!

HE'LL BE SO RELIEVED!

DAAADDY... DADDYYY!

THEY'RE HERE!

YOU GOT THEM!

YOU'RE GOING TO BE SO HAPPY!

WE KNEW YOU'D WANT 'EM RIGHT AWAY!

THE DADDY'S LITTLE GIRL HOLIDAY CATALOGUES.

CAZENOVE/WILL-AM

I TELL YOU, NAT. WENDY'S BEEN ACTING WEIRD LATELY.

FIRST, SHE PUT UP ALL THESE WEIRD POSTERS...

NEXT, SHE DOESN'T WANT TO PLAY WITH DOLLS OR PLAY HAIRDRESSER ANYMORE...

SHE DOESN'T DRESS LIKE SHE USED TO, AND SHE CHANGES OUTFITS, LIKE, EVERY 5 MINUTES...

SHE HOGS THE BATHROOM FOR HOURS, PUTTING TONS OF GUNK ON HER FACE...

LA LA LA

AND DIDJA NOTICE? SHE DOESN'T SMELL LIKE CANDY OR ICRE CREAM LIKE US ANYMORE. SHE WEARS *REAL* PERFUME.

YUP. MAKES MY EYES STING.

I'M TELLIN' YA! WENDY'S NOT A *GIRL* ANYMORE!

FOR REAL!

CAZENOVE/WILLIAM

27

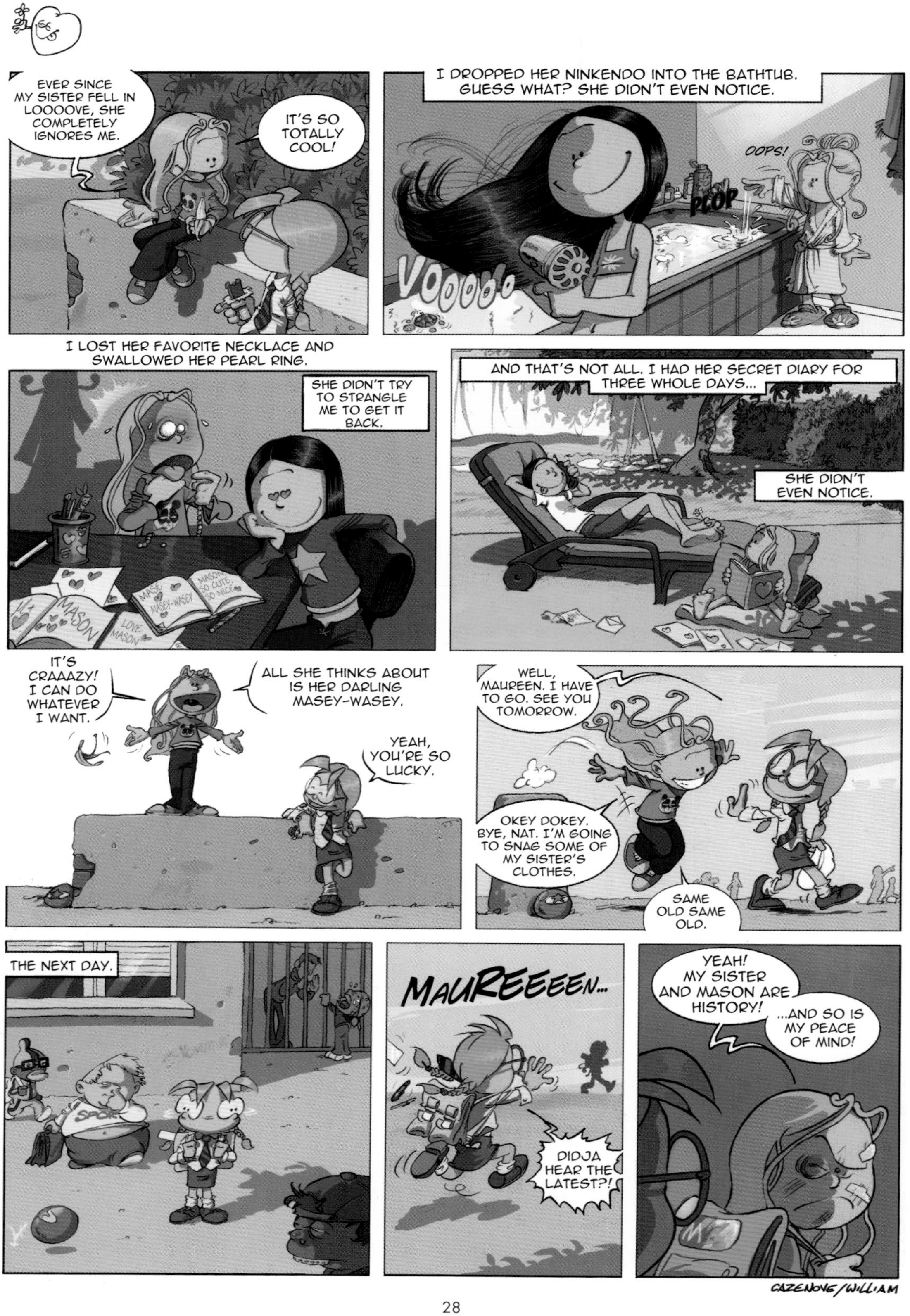
EVER SINCE MY SISTER FELL IN LOOOOVE, SHE COMPLETELY IGNORES ME.
IT'S SO TOTALLY COOL!
I DROPPED HER NINKENDO INTO THE BATHTUB. GUESS WHAT? SHE DIDN'T EVEN NOTICE.
OOPS!
PLOP
VOOOOO
I LOST HER FAVORITE NECKLACE AND SWALLOWED HER PEARL RING.
SHE DIDN'T TRY TO STRANGLE ME TO GET IT BACK.
MASON
LOVE MASON
MASE MASEY-WASEY
MASON SO CUTE, SO NICE
AND THAT'S NOT ALL. I HAD HER SECRET DIARY FOR THREE WHOLE DAYS...
SHE DIDN'T EVEN NOTICE.
IT'S CRAAAZY! I CAN DO WHATEVER I WANT.
ALL SHE THINKS ABOUT IS HER DARLING MASEY-WASEY.
YEAH, YOU'RE SO LUCKY.
WELL, MAUREEN. I HAVE TO GO. SEE YOU TOMORROW.
OKEY DOKEY. BYE, NAT. I'M GOING TO SNAG SOME OF MY SISTER'S CLOTHES.
SAME OLD SAME OLD.
THE NEXT DAY.
MAUREEEEEN...
DIDJA HEAR THE LATEST?!
YEAH! MY SISTER AND MASON ARE HISTORY!
...AND SO IS MY PEACE OF MIND!
CAZENOVE/WILLIAM

MY MOM HAD AN EXAM YESTERDAY.

OH YEAH?!

DID SHE PASS? DID YOU HELP HER STUDY FOR IT?!

WRONG KINDA TEST. A HOSPITAL THING.

THEY PUT YOU INTO A SCANNER AND LOOK INSIDE YOUR BODY!

OOH. THAT SOUNDS SCARY.

NUH-UH!

THEY CAN USE A SCANNER TO SEE YOUR BONES, MUSCLES, AND ALL THE OTHER THINGIES YOU HAVE INSIDE OF YOU. EVEN WHAT YOU ATE.

WOW

AND YOU DON'T HAVE TO TAKE OFF YOUR CLOTHES. IT SEES RIGHT THROUGH 'EM.

AND... IT SEES EVERY-THING?

YUP. EVERYTHING!

HEY... WHERE'RE YOU GOING, MAUREEN?

scanner

WAIT, SAY THAT AGAIN...

YOU WANT ME TO DO *WHAT* WITH YOUR NOTEBOOK?

NOT JUST ANY NOTEBOOK. IT'S MY SISTER'S *SECRET* DIARY!

CAZENOVE/WILLIAM

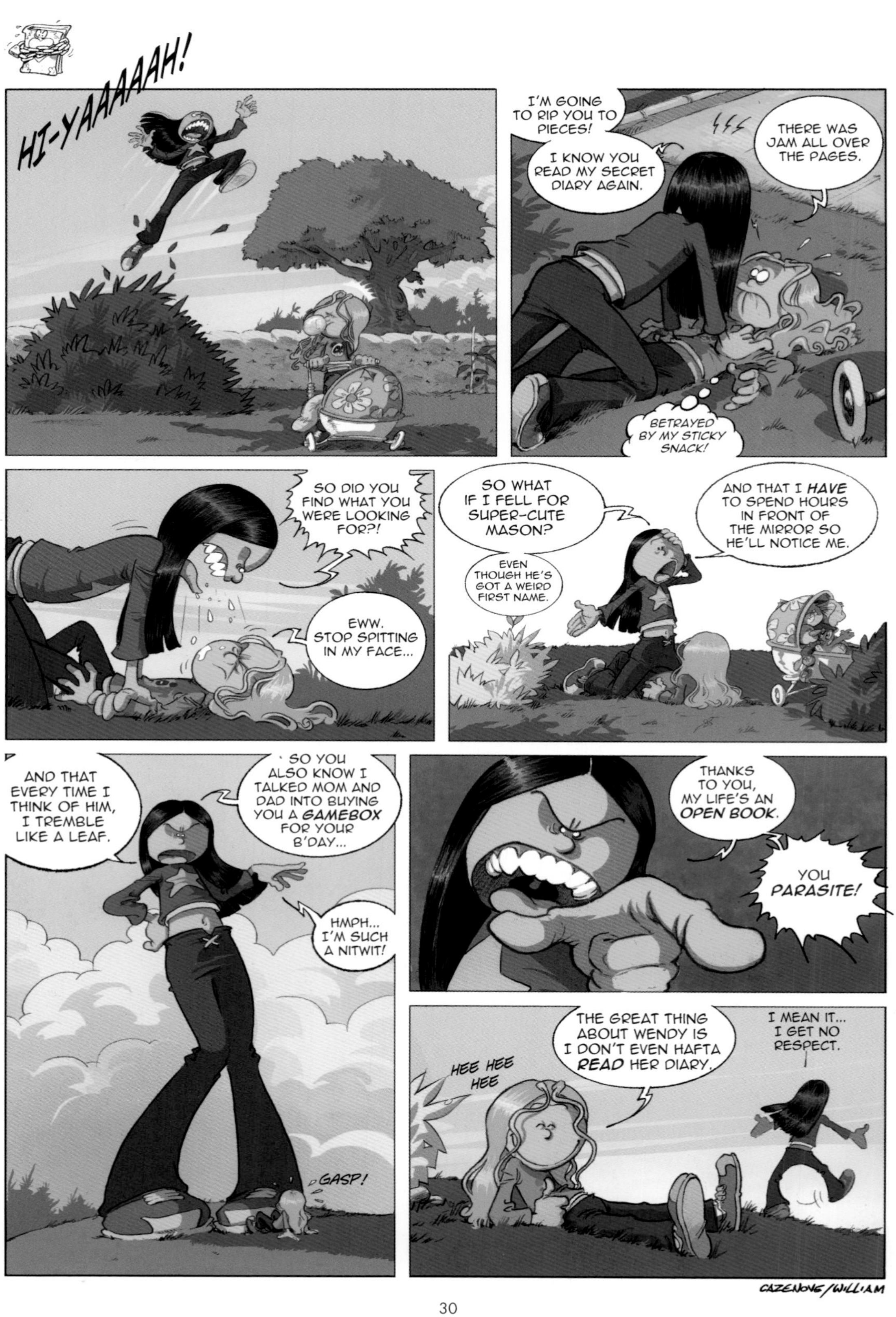
HI-YAAAAAH!
I'M GOING TO RIP YOU TO PIECES!
I KNOW YOU READ MY SECRET DIARY AGAIN.
THERE WAS JAM ALL OVER THE PAGES.
BETRAYED BY MY STICKY SNACK!
SO DID YOU FIND WHAT YOU WERE LOOKING FOR?!
EWW. STOP SPITTING IN MY FACE...
SO WHAT IF I FELL FOR SUPER-CUTE MASON?
EVEN THOUGH HE'S GOT A WEIRD FIRST NAME.
AND THAT I HAVE TO SPEND HOURS IN FRONT OF THE MIRROR SO HE'LL NOTICE ME.
AND THAT EVERY TIME I THINK OF HIM, I TREMBLE LIKE A LEAF.
SO YOU ALSO KNOW I TALKED MOM AND DAD INTO BUYING YOU A GAMEBOX FOR YOUR B'DAY...
HMPH... I'M SUCH A NITWIT!
GASP!
THANKS TO YOU, MY LIFE'S AN OPEN BOOK.
YOU PARASITE!
HEE HEE HEE
THE GREAT THING ABOUT WENDY IS I DON'T EVEN HAFTA READ HER DIARY.
I MEAN IT... I GET NO RESPECT.
CAZENOVE/WILLIAM

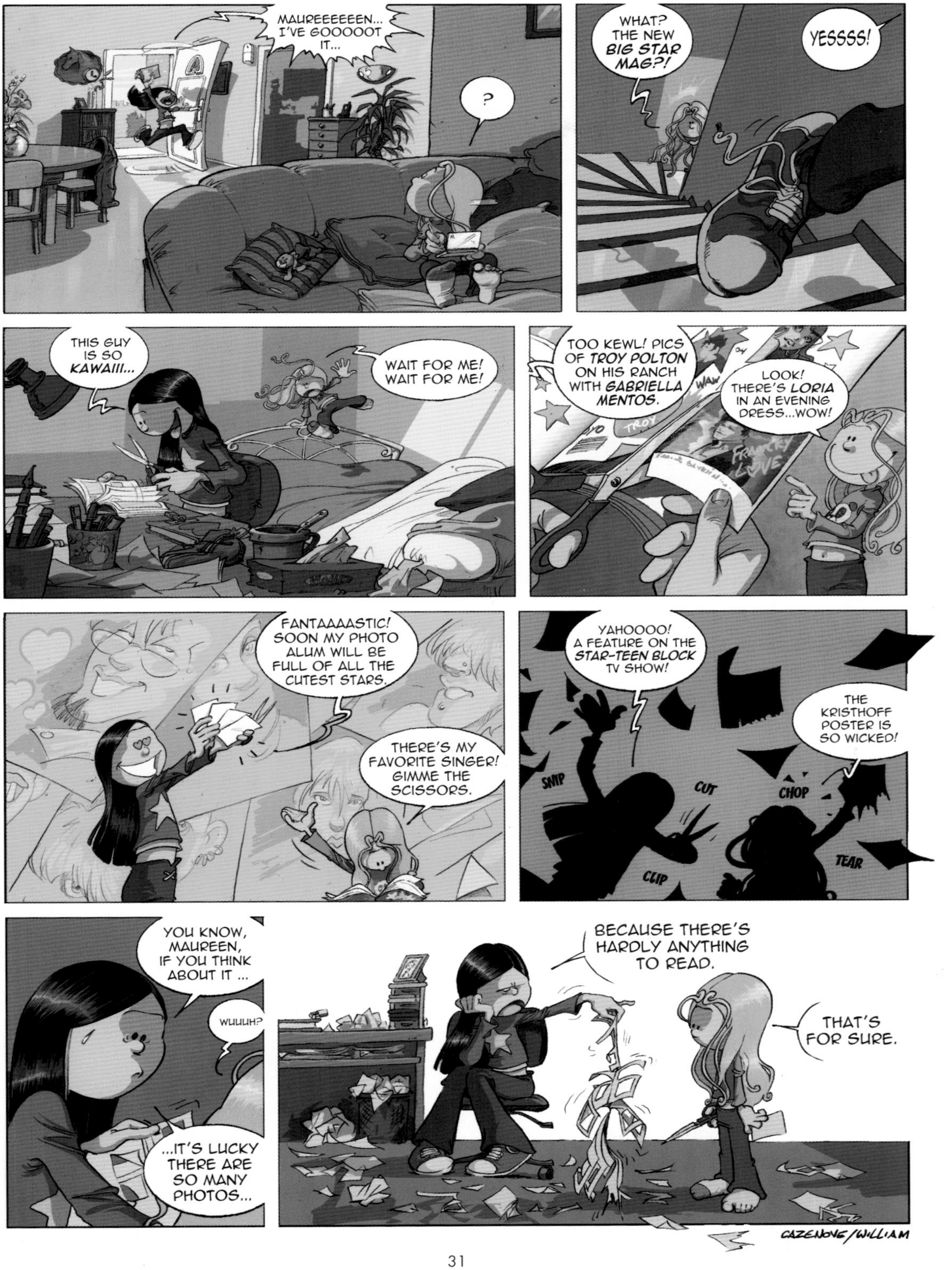
MAUREEEEEEN... I'VE GOOOOOT IT...
?
WHAT? THE NEW BIG STAR MAG?!
YESSSS!
THIS GUY IS SO KAWAIII...
WAIT FOR ME! WAIT FOR ME!
TOO KEWL! PICS OF TROY POLTON ON HIS RANCH WITH GABRIELLA MENTOS.
LOOK! THERE'S LORIA IN AN EVENING DRESS...WOW!
FANTAAAASTIC! SOON MY PHOTO ALUM WILL BE FULL OF ALL THE CUTEST STARS.
THERE'S MY FAVORITE SINGER! GIMME THE SCISSORS.
YAHOOOO! A FEATURE ON THE STAR-TEEN BLOCK TV SHOW!
THE KRISTHOFF POSTER IS SO WICKED!
SNIP
CUT
CHOP
CLIP
TEAR
YOU KNOW, MAUREEN, IF YOU THINK ABOUT IT ...
WUUUH?
...IT'S LUCKY THERE ARE SO MANY PHOTOS...
BECAUSE THERE'S HARDLY ANYTHING TO READ.
THAT'S FOR SURE.
CAZENOVE/WILLIAM

WHAT DO YOU WANT FOR DESSERT, MAUREEN?

LEMME DIG THROUGH MY SECRET STASH.

PFFFT. WHATEVS.

IF WE ONLY HAD STUFF THAT'S GOOD FOR YOU... YUCK.

AAAHHH... MY LOW-FAT YOGURT FOR MY *TOP MODEL* DIET!

THAT'S NOT LOW-FAT. IT'S CHOCK-FULL OF CREAM AND SUGAR.

HA HA HA

NO WAY! IT'S SUPER-FIT!

YUM NOM.... IT'S SO GOOOOD!

YUUUUUM

BUT THE CONTAINER SAYS IT ONLY HAS TWO CALORIES.

YOU SHOULD STAY AWAY FROM THAT STUFF IF YOU WANT TO STAY SKINNY.

TWO CALORIES?! MMMF, HEE HEE. YOU WERE LOOKING AT THE EXPIRATION DATE.

YOUR YOGURT'S *GONE BAD!*

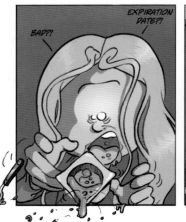

BAD?!

EXPIRATION DATE?!

IT'S OK, DAD. SHE'S IN TRAINING TO BE A *TOP MODEL.*

BLAAAAAAARGGHHH... GLARRGGH...

CAZENOVE/WILL'AM

MAUREEEEN...

WHY'RE YOU YELLING LIKE THAT?!

HELP! SAVE ME FROM THAT MONSTER... PLEEZE.

OH, YEEAAH. IT'S A REAL BEAUTY!

AND IT'S RIGHT OVER YOUR BED, TOO.

IT'LL LAY EGGS AND THEY'LL HATCH AND THEY'LL SWARM!

BUT I'M TOO SMALL TO REACH IT!

USE THE BROOM FROM THE GARDEN.

AND HURRY!

BLAH BLAH BLAH. PFFFFT. WHAT A WIMP.

HMMM. DO YOU WANT ME TO KILL IT?

EAT IT IF YOU WANT, BUT GET IT OUT OF MY ROOM.

OKAY OKAY OKAY!

THERE WE GO. PROBLEM SOLVED!

ALWAYS HAPPY TO HELP.

SHE OWES ME BIGTIME!

CAZENOVE/WILLIAM

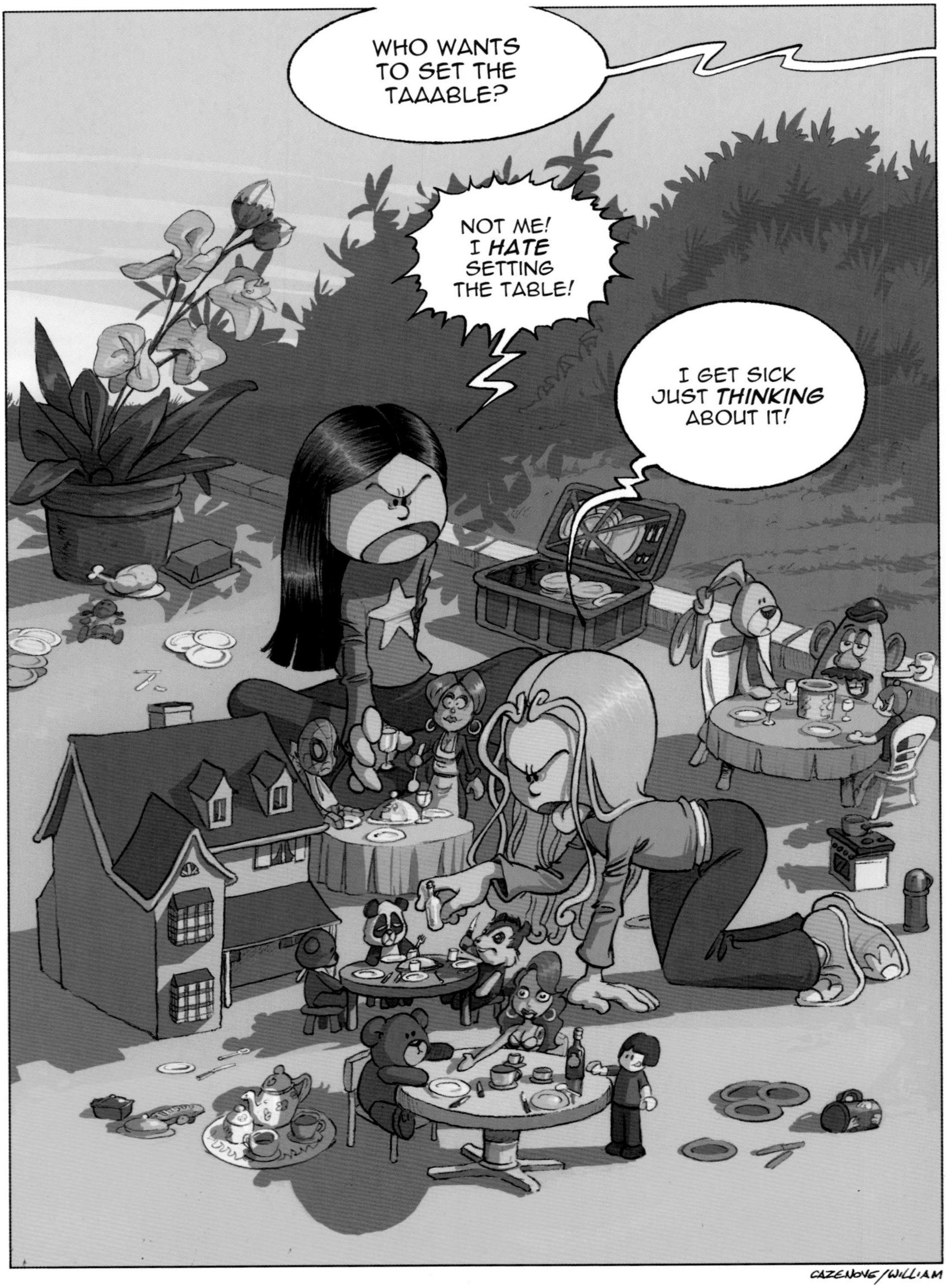

WHO WANTS TO SET THE TAAABLE?
NOT ME! I **HATE** SETTING THE TABLE!
I GET SICK JUST **THINKING** ABOUT IT!

CAZENOVE/WILLIAM

WOOOW! THE FIRST FLOWERS OF SPRING. THIS'LL MAKE AN AWESOME BOUQUET FOR MY TEACHER.

AND AN AWESOME PUNISHMENT IF WE'RE LATE TO SCHOOL.

WOOOW! TAKE A QUICK LOOK AT THESE WILD ROSES, WENDY.

HELP ME PICK SOME, PLEEEZE!

NO WAY. I'LL RUIN MY JACKET!

PFFT. COME ON, SISSY.

ALMOST THERE. ALMOST THERE ...

UH-OH. I'M STUCK!

HERE IT COMES!

STUPID THORNS!

AAAH! I HATE ROSES.

I GOT MY SWEATER ALL MESSED UP, AND I'M SUPER COOOOLD, TOO...

HERE YA GO— ALL BETTER NOW?

YES, SNIFF, THANKS, SNIFF...

YOU'RE A SUPER SISTER!

SO YOU FINALLY MANAGED TO SNAG HER NEW JACKET?!

NOW, THAT'S CLAAAAASSY!

YUP! MY PLAN WAS FOOLPROOF!

CAZENOVE/WILLIAM

WHEN I GROW UP, I'LL BE A STAR OF STAGE AND SCREEN.

IT'S SO AWESOME!

YEAAAH...

I'LL BE A STAR WHO *STAYS* AND *SCREAMS!*

OR MAYBE I'LL BE AN ICHTHYOLOGIST.

ME, TOO. I'LL BE AN ICK PEE-OLOGIST.

AND I CAN REALLY SEE MYSELF AS AN INTERIOR DECORATOR, TOO.

YEAAAH! MY DREAM CAREER... IN-THE-EAR DECORATOR!

HEY, WHOA! STOP ALWAYS COPYING ME, *SHRIMP!*

YOU'RE THE ONE ALWAYS COPYING ME FIRST.

FINE—BE THAT WAY! I'M GOING TO GO BE ALL BY MYSELF IN MY ROOM.

ME, TOO!

?!

WAAAAHH...

WENDY WON'T LET ME BE ALL BY MYSELF IN HER ROOM WITH HERRRRRR...

CAZENOVE/WILLIAM

36

HEY! WHAT'RE YOU DOING STILL OUTSIDE?

YOU SHOULD'VE GONE TO BED A LONG TIME AGO.

JUST A SEC...

WHAT NOW?

IT'S MY BUN BUN.

DON'T TELL ME YOU LOST IT AGAIN!

LAST TIME, WE SPENT THE WHOLE NIGHT LOOKING FOR IT.

LOL!

WE ALMOST HAD TO CALL IN THE COPS.

YOU EVEN DREW A POLICE SKETCH...

?

HEY! SHERLOCK! YOUR STINKY THINGY'S RIGHT HERE. NOW YOU CAN GO TO SLEEP.

HEY!

I KNOW WHERE HE IS, LAMEBRAIN...

I PUT HIM THERE MYSELF.

?? ???

HERE IT IS!

I WAS LOOKING FOR BUN BUN'S BUN BUN...

HE CAN'T SLEEP WITHOUT IT.

I CAN SLEEP FINE. *I'M* NOT A BABY ANYMORE.

CAZENOVE/WILLIAM

37

THERE'S NOTHING EASIER THAN PUTTING ON MAKEUP, WENDY.

I'LL EXPLAIN MY TECHNIQUE TO YOU.

CHIC!

OOH!

WOOOW...COOL, A **FREEBIE** MAKEUP CLASS.

AND AT NO CHARGE, TOO.

PUT SOME ROUGE ON YOUR FINGERTIP...

WHEN WENDY SEES WHAT AN EXPERT I AM, SHE'LL BE BLOWN AWAY.

DANG... I DIDN'T REALIZE IT WOULD BE SO COMPLICATED...

AHA! SPIFFY! THAT'S ALL I NEED...

IT'S SHOWTIME!

SO, SAMMIE, WHATCHA THINK?

FANTASTIC! I COULDN'T HAVE DONE IT BETTER MYSELF.

CLAP! CLAP!

IT'S SO FUNNY!

DIDN'T I TELL YOU, WENDY?!

HALLOWEEN MAKEUP IS MY SPECIALTY!

PUTTING ON GROWN-UP MAKEUP WAS EASY...!

CAZENOVE/WILLIAM

HOW CAN THEY TWIST THEMSELVES UP LIKE THAT?!

UNH! NAH, THAT'S NOT IT.

MAYBE IF YOU SWIVEL YOUR HIPS AROUND YOUR...

...WAISSSTTT...

SPLAT!

IT'S IMPOSSIBLE! WAIT—MAYBE THEY HELP EACH OTHER.

MAAAUREEEEEEN

I NEED YOU!

I HOPE IT'S IMPORTANT, 'CUZ I WAS SERIOUSLY BUSY UP THERE.

EEEK!

I DON'T BELIEVE IT!

IT *IS* POSSIBLE AFTER ALL!

WEHH?

CAZENOVE/WILLIAM

HEY, SAMMIE, WANT TO WATCH A DVD?!

SURE—WHY NOT?

WAIT, GIRLS...DON'T YOU WANT TO JUMP ROPE?

IT'LL BE FUN...

PRETTY PLEASE! PRETTY PLEASE! PRETTY PLEASE!

OKAY, OKAAAY! WE'LL JUMP ROPE.

SWIP!

IT'S YOUR TURN, MAUREEN.

COOL!

LOOK HOW GOOD I AM.

FASTER, MAUREEN.

FASTER, MAUREEN.

ARGGH

THERE WE GO. WE CAN GO WATCH THAT DVD IN PEACE AND QUIET.

YESSS!

CAZENOVE/WILLIAM

DING DING DONG

TRICK OR TREAT!

OOOOOOOO! A SCARY LITTLE WITCH! HERE YOU GO!

THANK YOU, MA'AM!

I'VE GOT CANDY! LOTS OF CANDY! I'VE GOT LOTS OF CANDY!

GET A MOVE ON! I DON'T WANT TO BE LATE TO AUDREY'S PARTY.

WILL MASEY-WASEY BE THERE?! OOOOO...SHE'S IN LOOOVE!

GGRRAAH... TRICK OR TREAT!

BRR...IT'S COLD.

ALL DONE? ABOUT TIME! *TWO HOURS* BEGGING AT ALL THE DOORS IN THE NEIGHBORHOOD. HMPH...

...YOU'RE SUCH A *BABY!*

ARGGGH... MY THROAT FEELS SCRATCHY...

GRAWK

SLURP

YUM CRACK

I'D LOVE TO GO TO AUDREY'S PARTY... JUST TO HEAR YOU CROAK AT MASON LIKE A FROG...

HEH HEH HEH

!?

I CROAK?!

LIKE A FROG...

— GRACKLE GRACKLLE

TRICK OR THROAT LOZENGES!

ARMACY

BAM!

BAM!

BAM!

HEY, WENDY, IT'S NOT AT ALL BELIEVABLE WITHOUT A COSTUME!

CAZENOVE/WILLIAM

41

SNIFF

SNIFF

?

SNIFF

SNIFF

?

SOMETHING IS REALLY STINKIN' UP YOUR ROOM!

OH, YEAH? MEBBE *YOU* STINK.

AHA! IT'S YOUR BUN BUN— IT *REEKS!*

PEEEYEWWW!

HOW CAN YOU SLEEP WITH THIS?

PEEYEWW!

APOLOGIZE TO BUN BUN RIGHT NOW!

PHOO

I'M *SO* SCARED. ANYWAY, I'M NOT GOING TO HURT YOUR STINKY BUN!

GIVE HIM BACK TO ME!

GIVE HIM!

GIMMMMEEE!

GET HIM OUT RIGHT NOW!

ANYWAY, HE DOESN'T STINK, SO THERE.

HE JUST SMELLS LIKE ME, THAT'S ALL!

LEMME OUT!

LEMME OUT!

CAZENOVE/WILLIAM

42

WHERE'RE YOU GOIN'?

AUDREY'S B'DAY PARTY.

TOO COOL! WAIT FOR ME, I'M COMING!

NO WAY. YOU'RE NOT INVITED.

BUUUT....I LIKE AUDREY, TOO.

YES, BUT YOU'RE NOT HER BESTIE.

SO WHAT? I'M GOING ANYWAY!

YOU WON'T GET IN.

LOL

WE'LL SEE ABOUT THAT!

MOVE IT!

HEY!

I'LL TELL YOU ALL ABOUT IT AFTER!

HA HA HA

HEH HEH

THE COAST IS CLEAR...

WE WON'T BE BOTHERED. WE CAN CELEBRATE AUDREY'S BIRTHDAY IN MY ROOM IN PEACE AND QUIET!

CAZENOVE/WILLIAM

43

YAY! SHOULD WE PLAY COSMIC COWBOY, WENDY?

SURE! I LOVED THE LAST EPISODE...

...THE EVIL SHERIFF ATTACKS BACK!!!

HI-YAAAH!

I'LL BE PRINCESS MUNKA.

IN YOUR DREAMS. I'M PRINCESS MUNKA.

PLUS SHE HAS BROWN HAIR, LIKE ME.

SCROUTCH!

KYYAH!

YES, BUT PRINCESS MUNKA DOES KARATE, LIKE THIS.

TOO DANGEROUS FOR YOU. YOU'LL KNOCK YOURSELF OUT. LET'S SAY YOU'LL BE KREMALIA INSTEAD.

SHE'S THE BEST!

NO WAY?! THAT'S SO LAME. KREMALIA NEVER HAS ANY FIGHT SCENES.

OKAY, THEN. YOU CAN BE ZHYNNA, THE PILOT.

ZHYNNA?! DO I LOOK LIKE A CRAZY BLONDE TO YOU?

SHE DRIVES A SPACE-TRASHCAN. SHE DOESN'T KNOW HOW TO FIGHT!

IF YOU WANT TO FIGHT, I CAN ARRANGE THAT.

LET GO OF ME, DIMBULB!

HEY OVER THERE! THAT'S ENOUGH OF THAT RACKET!

CALM DOWN OR I'LL SEND YOU BOTH TO YOUR ROOMS.

HEY, DADDY, WE AGREE ON ONE THING: YOU CAN BE THE EVIL SHERIFF!

YOU MAKE A GREAT VILLAIN!

CAZENOVE/WILLIAM

YIKES! MOM'LL GET MAD WHEN SHE FINDS OUT YOU'RE NOT DRESSED YET!

GRUMP... NOT MY FAULT. I'VE GOT NOTHING TO WEAR.

YOU MUST BE KIDDING!

YOU'VE GOT WAY MORE CLOTHES THAN ME!

HERE. JUST PUT ON THESE PANTS.

NOPE. THEY'RE TOO BLUE.

WEAR THIS, THEN.

NOPE! IT'S TOO TIGHT.

THE FRINGED TOP?

TOO MUCH FRINGE.

C'MON, ALREADY. IT'S JUST FOR ONE DAY!

I DON'T HAVE ANYTHING I LIIIIKE!

OKAY, SWEETIE. I HAVE AN IDEA...

DO YOU WANNA WEAR ANY OF MY CLOTHES?

YOU'RE STILL NOT READY, WENDY?

BUT... BUT...

JUST WHAT I WANTED!

CAZENOVE/WILLIAM

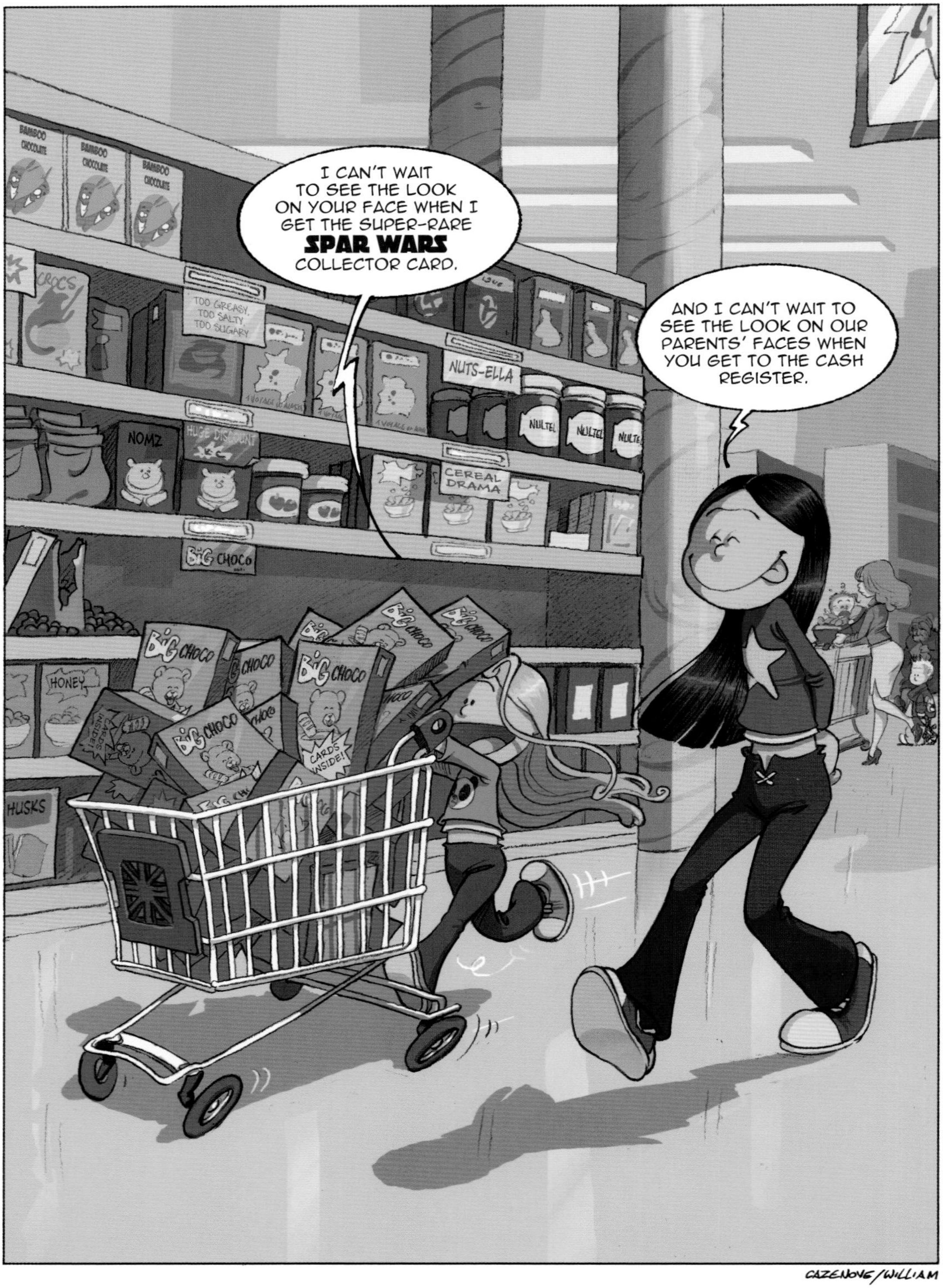
I CAN'T WAIT TO SEE THE LOOK ON YOUR FACE WHEN I GET THE SUPER-RARE **SPAR WARS** COLLECTOR CARD.
AND I CAN'T WAIT TO SEE THE LOOK ON OUR PARENTS' FACES WHEN YOU GET TO THE CASH REGISTER.
BAMBOO CHOCOLATE
CROCS
TOO GREASY. TOO SALTY. TOO SUGARY
NUTS-ELLA
NOMZ
HUGE DISCOUNT
NULTEL
CEREAL DRAMA
BIG CHOCO
HONEY
HUSKS
CARDS INSIDE!

CAZENOVE/WILLIAM

MOM, DAD, WE HAVE THE HONOR OF PRESENTING TO YOU...

THE SISTERS' SPRING AND SUMMER COLLECTION.

WE BEGIN THIS SHOW WITH A SWEATER AND SHORT SKIRT SET THAT WENDY ALREADY WORE WHEN SHE WAS MY AGE.

T-SHIRT WITH HOLES UNDER THE ARMS.

TOO-FADED, TOO-TIGHT JEANS.

A JACKET THAT'S NOT SHABBY-CHIC—JUST SHABBY.

HAND-ME-DOWN MAXI SKIRT FROM MOM.

VINTAGE RUNNING SUIT WITH MOLDY SNEAKERS.

WITH MAYONNAISE-STAIN DECORATION.

THANK YOU!

THANK YOU!

MESSAGE RECEIVED! WE'LL GO BUY YOU SOME CLOTHES.

WELL PLAYED!

LIKE-WISE!

CAZENOVE/WILLIAM

WHEN I'M BIG, I'LL BE LIVING HAPPILY IN A BEAUTIFUL VILLA ON THE OUTSKIRTS OF A PRETTY FOREST...WITH A POOL, A BIG GARDEN, AND ALL THAT...

...I'LL LIVE WITH MY SWEETHEART... WE'LL BE DEEPLY IN LOVE WITH EACH OTHER...

WENDY, DARLING...

MASEY-WASEY, MY LOVE...

ALSO, I'LL HAVE LOTS OF DIFFERENT TYPES OF ANIMALS, IN ALL DIFFERENT COLORS...

...I'LL WORK IN MEDICAL RESEARCH. I'LL DISCOVER LOTS OF VACCINES TO CURE EVERY ILLNESS.

YES, MR. PRESIDENT. I DISCOVERED A VACCINE FOR TOOTHACHES, TOO. WHAT WOULD YOU LIKE ME TO DO NEXT?

MALARIA
SMALLPOX
MIGRAINES
MUMPS
HAIR LOSS

AND I'LL DEVOTE ALL MY FREE TIME TO MY FAVORITE HOBBY: INTERIOR DESIGN.

BLEU

I'LL DO IT! I'LL DO IT!

?!

I'LL USE THE SAME COLORS I USED IN *MY* HOUSE!

IT'LL ROCK!

HOW DARE YOU RUIN THE WHOLE REST OF MY LIFE LIKE THAT?!

???

CAZENOVE/WILLIAM

48

2: A Style of Our Own

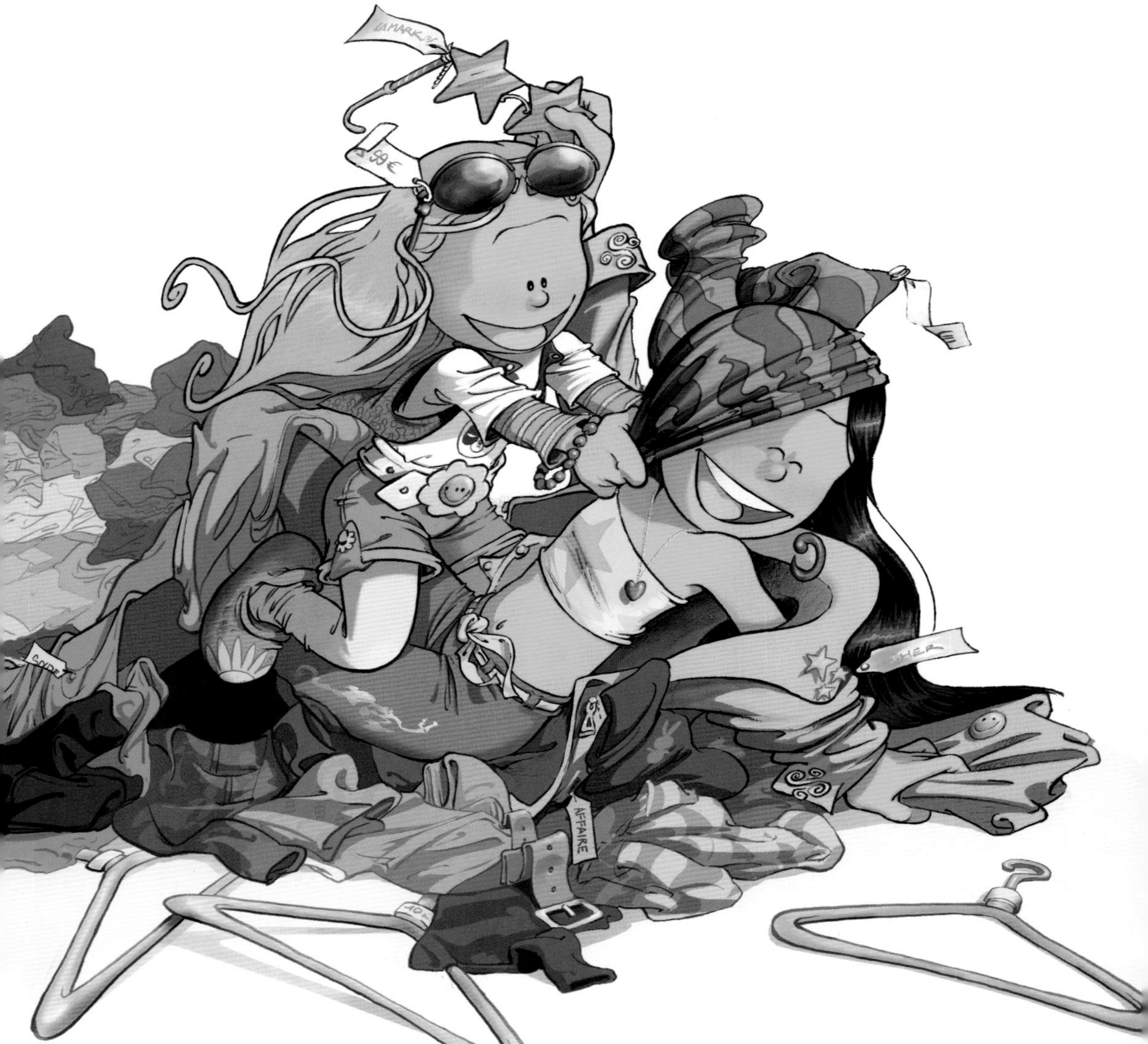
AFFAIRE

HEAD AND SHOULDERS, KNEES AND TOES, KNEES AND TOE-OE-OE-OES

HEY, DIVA, WILL YOU BE *DONE* SOON?

CHILL! I'M ALREADY DONE!

?!

YOU'VE BEEN HOGGING THE DRESSING ROOM...

...JUST TO TRY ON *SHOES?!*

IT'S NOT MY FAULT I HAVE SHY TOES.

WHAT A WASTE OF TIME!

WELL, *YOU'RE* A WASTE OF SPACE!

GRRRRR...

MOVE ASIDE, SHRIMP!

BOP!

I'VE GOT ACTUAL *CLOTHING* TO TRY ON!

BA-DA-BLAM!

SO IT'S OKAY FOR *YOU* TO HOG THE DRESSING ROOM JUST TO TRY ON A HEADBAND?

SALE

CAZENOVE/WILLIAM

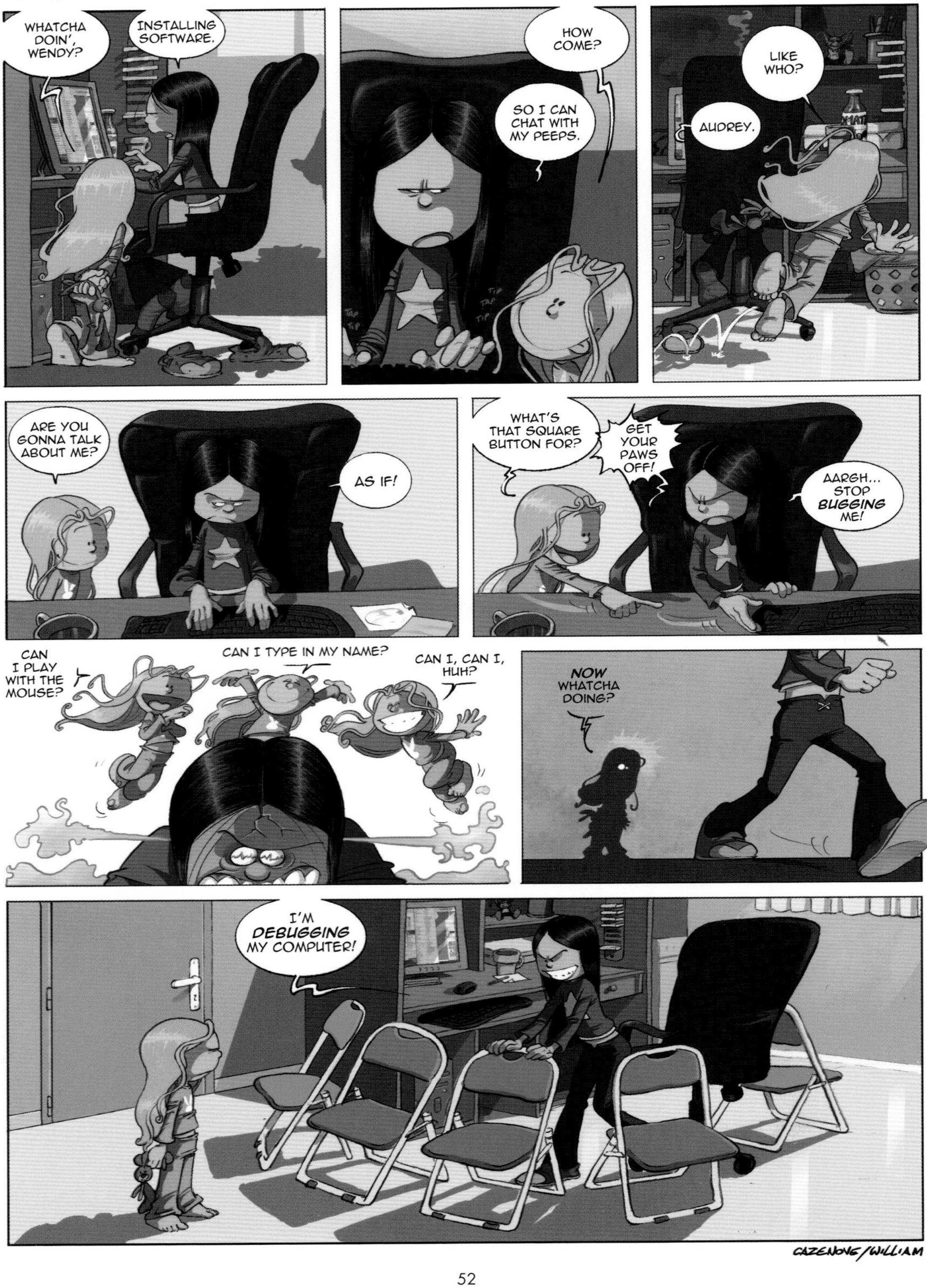

WHATCHA DOIN', WENDY?
INSTALLING SOFTWARE.
HOW COME?
SO I CAN CHAT WITH MY PEEPS.
LIKE WHO?
AUDREY.
ARE YOU GONNA TALK ABOUT ME?
AS IF!
WHAT'S THAT SQUARE BUTTON FOR?
GET YOUR PAWS OFF!
AARGH... STOP BUGGING ME!
CAN I PLAY WITH THE MOUSE?
CAN I TYPE IN MY NAME?
CAN I, CAN I, HUH?
NOW WHATCHA DOING?
I'M DEBUGGING MY COMPUTER!

CAZENOVE/WILLIAM

WE HAVE A HIDEOUT IN THE WOODS, WHERE WE CAN TAKE A BREAK FROM OUR PARENTS.

TO GET THERE, WE CROSS A MEADOW FULL OF FLOWERS.

WHILE THE PRETTY BIRDS FROLIC NEARBY...

AND THE PLANTS GROW LUXURIOUSLY.

ANIMALS ROAM FREELY...

...NEAR A PEACEFUL STREAM.

WHEN ALL IS SAID AND DONE, WE ACTUALLY LIKE STAYING HOME.

WE NEED A BREAK FROM OUR BREAK!

CAZENOVE/WILL'AM

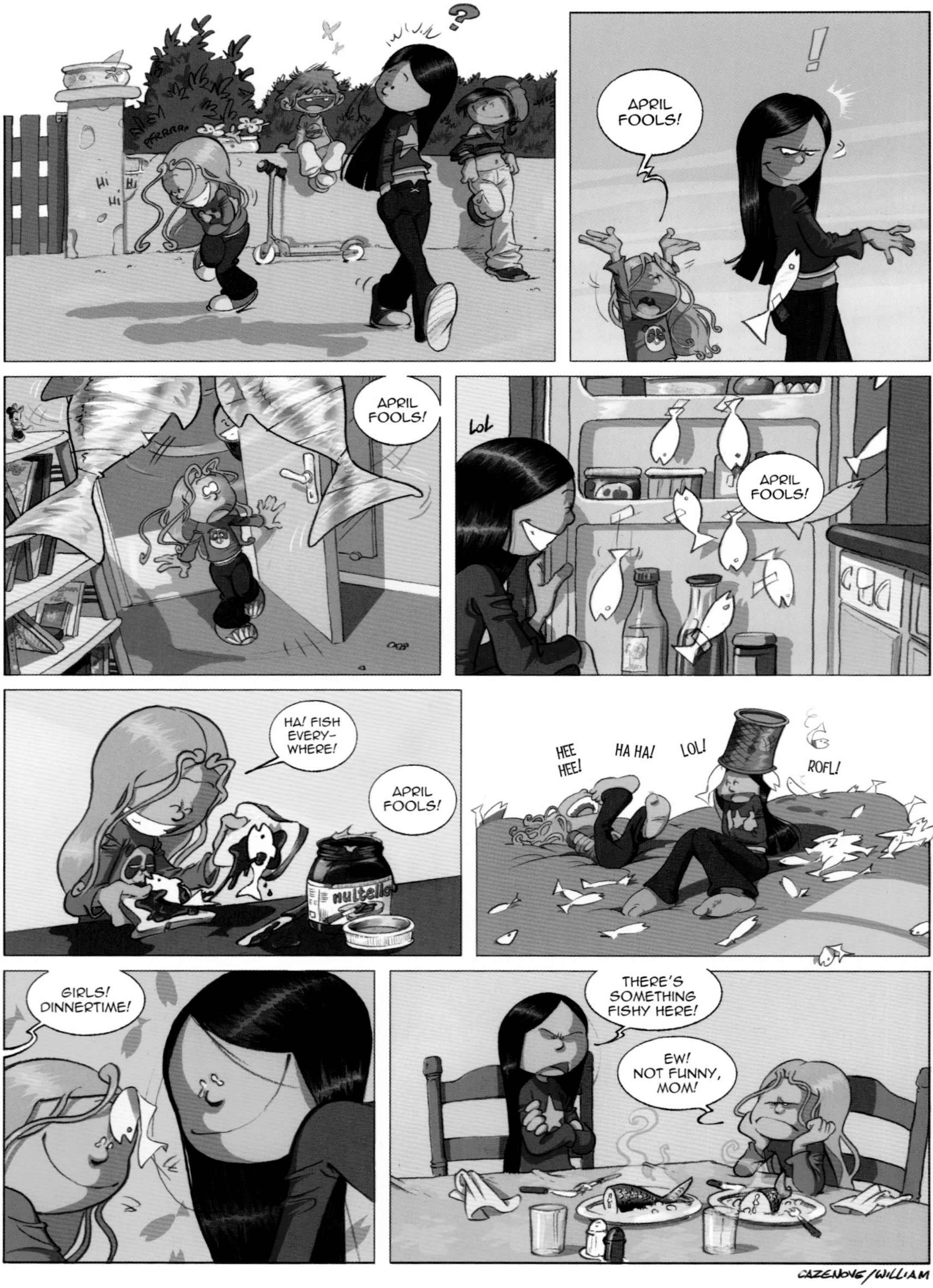
HI
HI
HI
APRIL FOOLS!
APRIL FOOLS!
LOL
APRIL FOOLS!
HA! FISH EVERY-WHERE!
APRIL FOOLS!
HEE HEE!
HA HA!
LOL!
ROFL!
GIRLS! DINNERTIME!
THERE'S SOMETHING FISHY HERE!
EW! NOT FUNNY, MOM!
CAZENOVE/WILLIAM

C'MON, MAUREEN, NO CHICKENING OUT!

WHO'S FIRST?

GO ON!

UH, WENDY... YOU'RE SURE IT WON'T HURT?

I'VE TOLD YOU AGAIN AND AGAIN! YOU'RE JUST BEING A SCAREDY-CAT!

HEY! DON'T PUSH ME! AND I'M *NOT* A SCAREDY-CAT!

PROMO 5 TATTOOS = 1 PIERCING FREE!

IT'S JUST A TEENY-TINY HOLE MADE WITH A TEENY-TINY NEEDLE. NO BIG DEAL!

TRUST YOUR BIG SISTER. IT WON'T HURT AT ALL!

SEE ?!!

IT'LL BE OVER BEFORE YOU KNOW IT, SWEETIE.

OKAY...

THERE... YOU'RE DONE!

SO... DID IT HURT?

NAH, NOT AT ALL. IT BARELY STUNG.

YOU WERE RIGHT!

GREAT! *NOW* YOU CAN DO MINE!

CAZENOVE/WILLIAM

WHATCHA DOING WITH DADDY'S HELMET?

DO YOU HAVE A HEAD COLD?

HA, HA. LEAVE ME ALONE, SHRIMP.

ARE YOU DRYING YOUR HAIR?

LISTENING TO MUSIC?

HIDING YOUR UGLY FACE?

NAH, BRAT. I'M HAVING A HUGE ACNE OUTBREAK RIGHT NOW. WANNA SEE?

EW! GET AWAY FROM ME!

IT'S HARD TO GO OUT WITH A HUGE ZIT RIGHT ON THE TIP OF MY NOSE.

WHY DON'T YOU POP IT?

DON'T HAVE TO! MOM GOT ME **THIS** AT THE DRUGSTORE. IT'S SUPPOSED TO MAKE ALL YOUR ZITS DISAPPEAR.

STOP/SPOT

TOO COOL!

TOO COOL!

WAIT A SEC— IN JUST TWO DAYS MY SISTER GOT RID OF HER WHOLE HACKNEY OUT-TAKE...

IT SHOULD WORK ON YOU, TOO!

CAZENOVE/WILLIAM

MAUREEN, SEE THE BAD SCRATCH I GOT IN THE BUSHES YESTERDAY?

HMPH! I GO THROUGH THE BUSHES EVERY DAY...

LET ME SHOW YOU SOME *REAL* OWIES!

SO, THIS SCAR ON MY KNEE IS FROM WHEN I CRASHED MY SISTER'S BIKE...

I DIDN'T EVEN CRY.

THESE SCABS ON MY ELBOW ARE FROM A NASTY FALL IN THE BATHROOM...

WENDY LEAVES HER STUFF LYING AROUND, Y'KNOW.

I GOT THIS BIG BRUISE ON MY LEG FROM A KITCHEN CHAIR...

...THAT WAS IN THE WRONG PLACE.

BUT WORST OF ALL IS THE HUGE LUMP THAT WENDY GAVE ME WHEN I BUSTED HER NINTENDO.

THAT MUST REALLY HURT!

WAIT... I DON'T SEE ANY LUMP?!

THAT'S 'CAUSE SHE HASN'T NOTICED YET.

CAZENOVE/WILLIAM

LA LA LA
I'M CLEO, THE MOST BEAUTIFUL
OF ALL THE MERMAIDS
THE PRETTIEST AND
THE CLEVEREST...

LA LA LA LA
C'MON C'MON,
LET'S SHAMPOO

AAAAAAAAAAA*AAAAAAAAAAAAAAAAAA

MY
EYES!

OWWWWW!
IT BUUUURNS!
I CAN'T
SEEEEEEEEE!

I'M GONNA
BE BLIND AND
IT'S ALL YOUR
FAULT!

I HAVEN'T
EVEN PUT ANY
SHAMPOO IN
YOUR HAIR YET,
GENIUS.

SO STOP
CRYING!

YEAH,
I KNOW
...

WELL, NOW YOU
KNOW WHAT'LL
HAPPEN IF YOU GET
EVEN A SINGLE DROP
IN MY EYES.

Squeeze!

Squeeze!

Grumble

PLORCH!

CAZENOVE/WILLIAM

ANYONE WANT TO HELP ME MAKE DINNER?

DO *YOU* WANNA GO IN THERE?

HECK, NO! IT'S WAY TOO DANGEROUS!

REMEMBER WHAT IT WAS LIKE SLICING ONIONS?

AND WHEN WE HAD TO CHOP VEGETABLES?

COUP!

FRYING THE FRIES WAS THE WORST.

PCHIII!

I'LL NEVER FORGET THAT CASSEROLE!

OWWWW!

AND THE DISASTER WITH THE BLENDER.

DID YOU PUT THE LID ON?

IT NEEDS A LID?

BUT THE MOST DANGEROUS THING IS... *THE FOOD ITSELF.*

IT'S TURNIP STEW. IT'S VERY TASTY AND *VERY* GOOD FOR YOU!

I SAW IT MOVE!

CAZENOVE/WILLIAM

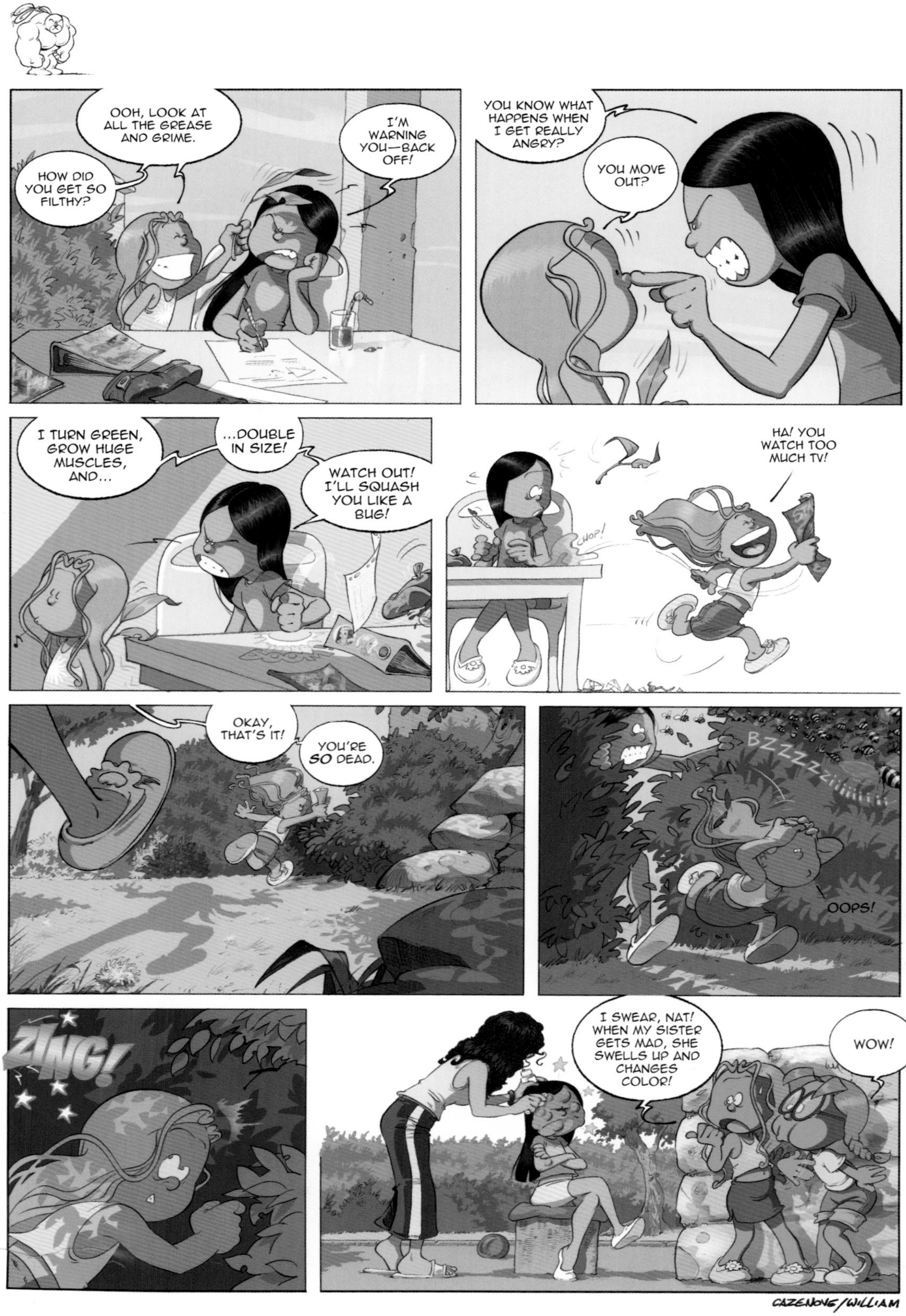

OOH, LOOK AT ALL THE GREASE AND GRIME.
HOW DID YOU GET SO FILTHY?
I'M WARNING YOU—BACK OFF!
YOU KNOW WHAT HAPPENS WHEN I GET REALLY ANGRY?
YOU MOVE OUT?
I TURN GREEN, GROW HUGE MUSCLES, AND...
...DOUBLE IN SIZE!
WATCH OUT! I'LL SQUASH YOU LIKE A BUG!
CHOP!
HA! YOU WATCH TOO MUCH TV!
OKAY, THAT'S IT!
YOU'RE SO DEAD.
BZZZZZ
OOPS!
ZING!
I SWEAR, NAT! WHEN MY SISTER GETS MAD, SHE SWELLS UP AND CHANGES COLOR!
WOW!
CAZENOVE/WILLIAM

SO, WHAT'S MASON GETTING YOU FOR VALENTINE'S DAY?

NOTHING, I GUESS.

WHADDAYA MEAN, NOTHING?

HE HASN'T SAID A THING.

YOU'RE KIDDING!

ANY BOY WHO HELD MY HAND AND KISSED ME HAD BETTER GET ME SOMETHING *NICE* FOR VALENTINE'S DAY.

IF NOT— I'D KICK HIM TO THE CURB.

REALLY? YOU WOULD?

YOU BET! I'D DUMP HIM IN A NANOSECOND!

C'MERE, HANDSOME!

???

SMACK!

GET ME A VIDEO GAME FOR VALENTINE'S DAY, OR I'LL DUMP YOU—

???

—ON A NANNY- SOCCER!

CAZENOVE/WILLIAM

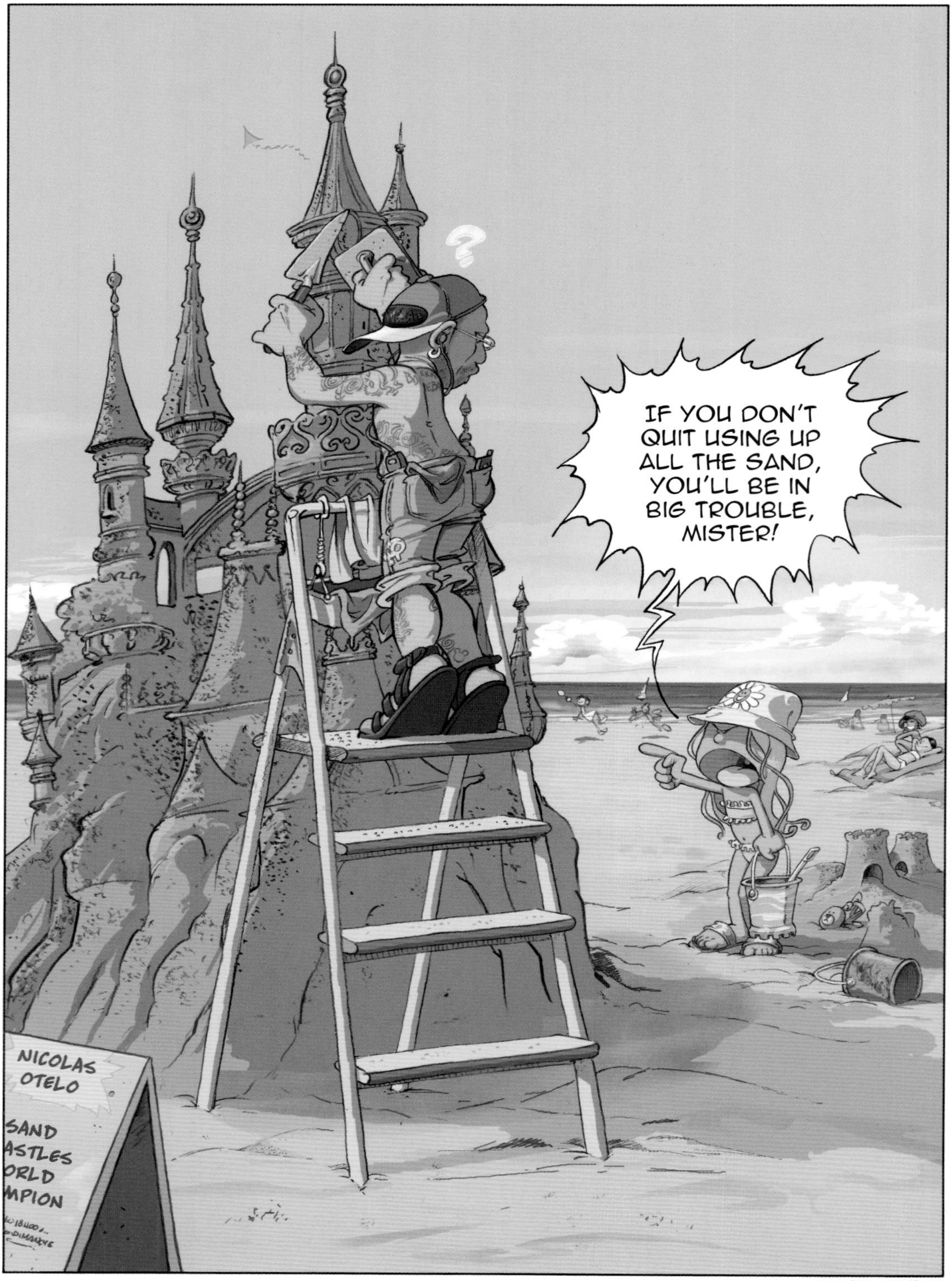
IF YOU DON'T QUIT USING UP ALL THE SAND, YOU'LL BE IN BIG TROUBLE, MISTER!
NICOLAS OTELO
SAND

CAZENOVE/WILLIAM

WENDY! HEY, WENDY!

WHATCHA THINK—DO GREEN AND PINK GO TOGETHER?

HEY! I'M TRYING TO GET A TAN HERE!

STOP BLOCKING MY SUN!

COME ON, WENDY! IT'S OUR DUTY TO PASS ON FASHION SENSE TO THE YOUNGER GENERATION.

PFFFT... GO AHEAD. KNOCK YOURSELF OUT.

THE MOST IMPORTANT THING IS TO CHOOSE HUES THAT COMPLEMENT YOUR COLORING ...

HAIR, CLOTHES, AND MAKEUP SHOULD ALL COORDINATE.

ALL THE TIME?

TOTALLY! TO BE FASHIONABLE, YOUR SHOES SHOULD GO WITH YOUR TOP, YOUR SKIRT WITH YOUR PURSE, AND YOUR SCRUNCHIE WITH YOUR SOCKS.

YES!

THAT'S THE STYLE?

SO DO PINK AND GREEN GO WELL TOGETHER?

CERTAINLY— THEY'RE ALL THE RAGE!

THANKS A LOT, SAMMIE!

GO FOR IT, NAT! MIXING PISTACHIO AND RASPBERRY IS THE LATEST STYLE!

CAZENOVE/WILLIAM

63

WHEEEEEE!

AREN'TCHA GONNA SWIM WITH YOUR FAVORITE SISTER?

OWWWWW!

ARE YOU NUTS? I TOLD YOU YESTERDAY THAT I GOT A MEGA SUNBURN ON MY BACK.

OH! I FORGOT...

I'M SOOOO SORRY, WENDY! CAN YOU EVER FORGIVE ME?

OWWWW

I BURNED MY ARMS, TOOOO!

SO I CAN'T TOUCH YOU AT ALL?

THAT'S RIGHT! NOW LEAVE ME ALONE!

OKAY! SEE YA LATER!

THWACK!

OOPS...

HEY! MAUREEN! DIDJA KNOW YOU GOT A SUNBURN ON YOUR BUTT?

CAZENOVE/WILLIAM

CAN YOU DRAW ME A PICTURE?

NO WAY! I CAN'T EVEN DRAW STICK FIGURES!

BUT IT'S EASY... WATCH...

TA-DA! IT'S A PORTRAIT OF YOU, I SWEAR!

ALL I HAD TO DO WAS ARRANGE A LOT OF ZITS ON A HUGE POTATO.

NICE!

HERE'S ONE FROM A BIRD'S-EYE VIEW.

I JUST NEED TWO GREAT BIG CIRCLES FOR YOUR FEET AND ONE REALLY SMALL ONE FOR YOUR HEAD.

HUMPH!

AND HERE YOU ARE RIDING A BIKE...

THE BIKE IS ALL TWISTED UP 'CAUSE YOU'RE SO FAT.

LOL

ROFL

GRRRR

I'M GOING TO TWIST UP YOUR FACE!

TOUCHY, TOUCHY!

NO, WE HAVEN'T SEEN HER.

AND SHE SAYS SHE CAN'T DRAW!

CAZENOVE/WILLIAM

THREE BOUNCES! I BROKE THE RECORD!

MY TURN!

KER-PLUM

GRR... GRUMBLE GRUMBLE

HA HA! UNDERWATER BOUNCES DON'T COUNT!

DON'T WORRY, MAUREEN...

LET ME SHOW YOU HOW. FIRST, YOU CHOOSE A NICE FLAT STONE...

SWEET!

THEN YOU THROW IT AS HARD AS YOU CAN!

UFF!

WOW!

THANKS, WENDY! LET ME TRY NOW!

FOUR BOUNCES! YOU SMASHED THE RECORD!

SPLOOSH!

CAZENOVE/WILLIAM

66

I HAVE TO RETURN THESE BOOKS TO THE LIBRARY.

BUT I WANNA GO WIIIITH YOU!

HEY! TAKE ME TOO!

NO, NO, NO! YOU TWO STAY HERE AND BUY VEGGIES FOR DINNER TONIGHT.

SO LAME!!!

EWWW! VEGGIES! YUCK!

BUT, MOM!

NO BUTS. IF YOU PICK THEM OUT YOURSELVES, YOU'LL HAVE NO EXCUSE NOT TO EAT THEM.

MOMMY! PLEEEZE!

WE'VE GOT TO FIND SOMETHING OR WE'LL BE IN SERIOUS TROUBLE.

BUT THEY LOOK SO GROSS!

HEY, MAUREEN... TAKE A LOOK OVER HERE!

SPIF-FY-TAS-TIC!

WHAT WERE YOU THINKING?! THESE VEGETABLES ARE ALL MOLDY!

REALLY? ARE YOU SURE? WE THOUGHT THEY LOOKED CUTE. LIKE STUFFED ANIMALS.

DOES THIS MEAN WE'RE EATING AT BURGER BASKET TONIGHT?

CAZENOVE/WILLIAM

WHAT ARE YOU DOING?

YOU'RE SUPPOSED TO KICK THE BALL INTO THE *NET!*

I KNOW! BUT IT'S MORE FUN TO KICK IT AT THE GOALKEEPER!

CAZENONE/WILLIAM

I LIKE TO EAT, EAT, EAT APPLES AND BANANAS

♪ I LIKE TO ATE, ATE, ATE, AY-PLES AND BA-NAY-NAYS

I LIKE TO ITE, ITE, ITE, I-PLES AND BA-NI-NI'S!

♪ I LIKE TO OTE, OTE, OTE, O-PLES AND BA-NO-NOS!

WHY DID I EVER TEACH HER THAT SONG?

MOM, DO SOMETHING! SHE'S DRIVING ME CRAZY. I CAN'T TAKE IT ANY MORE!

SHE'S BEEN STUCK ON *REPEAT* SINCE YESTERDAY.

I KNOW, WENDY! I'M ABOUT TO SNAP, MYSELF!

SNAG!

GRRR!

I LIKE TO OOT, OOT, OOT, OO-PLES AND BA-NOO-NOOS!

IF I DON'T THINK OF SOMETHING...

SHE'LL NEVER STOP—NEVER EVER EVER!!!

I'VE *GOT* IT!

PAF!

EEEWW! YUCK! APPLESAUCE!

WHY CAN'T I HAVE FRIES LIKE YOU?

SHE STILL DOESN'T GET IT!

CAZENOVE/WILLIAM

69

I ABSOLUTELY LOVE THESE COSTUMES MOM MADE FOR US!

YEAH— THEY'RE WAY TOO COOL!

I FEEL *INVINCIBLE* WHEN I PUT IT ON.

ARE WE GOING TO THE SHACK?

YOU BET! AND WE'LL HAVE TO TACKLE A TRIBE OF TROLLS ON THE WAY!

DON'T FORGET THE DRAGON WE NEED TO SKEWER!

WE CAN BE THE GUARDIANS OF THE FOREST IN THESE OUTFITS!

YES! THEY GIVE US *LOADS* OF SUPERPOWERS!

BETTER HIDE, BAD GUYS! HERE COME THE SUPER SISTERS!

WHERE ARE YOU GOING?

THE OLD SHACK IN THE WOODS.

YOU WANNA COME WITH?

YIKES! THE SH-SH-SH- SHACK?

MY MOTHER WON'T LET ME GO THERE.

SHE SAYS A WITCH LIVES THERE.

WITH FINGERNAILS LIKE CLAWS AND LOTS OF HAIRY WARTS.

REALLY ???

— GULP!

UM, MOM... THIS COSTUME ISN'T REALLY WORKING OUT FOR ME AFTER ALL.

SAME HERE, YEP.

IT'S... NOT FLATTERING ON ME.

CAZENOVE/WILLIAM

I DON'T WANNA TAKE OUT THE TRA-A-ASH!!!

IT'S STINKY! IT'S LEAKY! IT'S GROSS!

I THINK IT'S MEGA FUN!!!

TAKING OUT THE TRASH... MEGA FUN ???

OF COURSE! IF YOU THROW THE BAG LIKE A BASKETBALL PLAYER...

DUNK!

NOTHING BUT NET!

OR, PRETEND YOU'RE A SNIPER...

BUT YOU ONLY GET ONE CHANCE, OR YOUR MISSION WILL FAIL!

POW!

BUT MY FAVORITE

IS TO DO IT

SUPER W STYLE!

I'M GONNA KICK A FIELD GOAL WITH IT!

RIGHT THROUGH THE UPRIGHTS!

WHOMP!

LOOKS LIKE YOU'RE GONNA BE BATTING CLEAN-UP!

AND DON'T EXPECT *ME* TO PLAY FOLLOW THE LEADER!

CAZENOVE/WILL·AM

HEY! WHAT'S WRONG WITH YOU?

GUESS WHAT, MAUREEN?

UH...YOU'VE LOST YOUR MIND?

I'M WORKING ON MY NEW DANCE ROUTINE.

SOON IT'LL BE PERFECT.

YOU'VE GOT A LONG WAY TO GO.

I'LL DO IT WHEREVER AND...

...WHENEVER I WANT.

AFTER ALL, I MIGHT BE SPOTTED BY AN AGENT...

UH... SURE.

CRUNCH! CHOMP!

HEY YOU! WHAT DO YOU THINK YOU'RE DOING?

YOUR DAUGHTER WAS MAKING FUN OF ME WHILE I WAS DIRECTING TRAFFIC.

SPOTTED BY AN AGENT, YEP!

CAZENOVE/WILLIAM

HOORAY! WE'RE GOING TO WATCH A HORROR MOVIE

NOT SO FAST! IT'S RATED *AGE 10 AND UP*, SO YOU CAN'T WATCH IT.

TIME FOR BEDDY-BYE, KIDDO!

HEY, WHAT IF I ONLY WATCH HALF? THAT SHOULD BE OKAY FOR KIDS *AGE 5 AND UP...*

NO, NO, AND NO! YOU'LL BE TOO SCARED!

IT'S NOT FAIR!

THERE ARE ZOMBIES...

SLIMY MONSTERS...

BLOOD EVERYWHERE. YUCK. AND TEDDY BEARS...

...WITH THEIR HEADS CHOPPED OFF!

THERE'S A GIRL WITH MONSTERS UNDER HER BED...

AN OGRE WITH A HUGE SPIKED CLUB...

AND A WEREWOLF WITH LOTS OF SHARP TEETH.

MOOOMMYYYYY...

WENDY, YOU KNOW BETTER THAN TO SCARE YOUR LITTLE SISTER LIKE THAT!

BUT, MOM, SHE WAS THE ONE WHO...

WHAT'S GOING ON WITH YOUR SISTER???

DON'T GO NEAR HER. SHE'S RATED KIDS AGE 10 AND UP!

CAZENOVE/WILLIAM

73

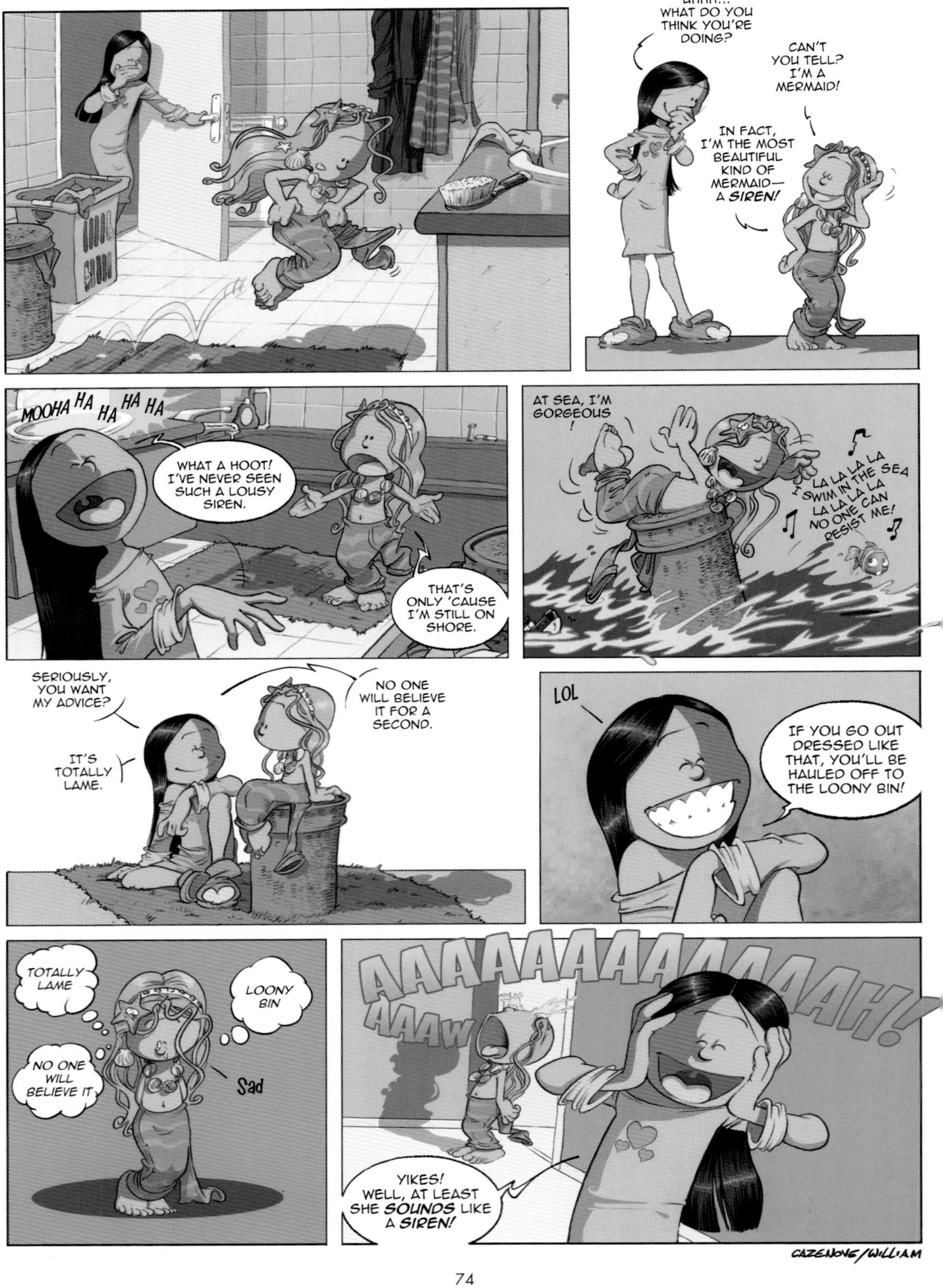
UHHH... WHAT DO YOU THINK YOU'RE DOING?
CAN'T YOU TELL? I'M A MERMAID!
IN FACT, I'M THE MOST BEAUTIFUL KIND OF MERMAID— A SIREN!
MOOHA HA HA HA HA
WHAT A HOOT! I'VE NEVER SEEN SUCH A LOUSY SIREN.
THAT'S ONLY 'CAUSE I'M STILL ON SHORE.
AT SEA, I'M GORGEOUS!
LA LA LA LA I SWIM IN THE SEA LA LA LA LA NO ONE CAN RESIST ME!
SERIOUSLY, YOU WANT MY ADVICE?
IT'S TOTALLY LAME.
NO ONE WILL BELIEVE IT FOR A SECOND.
LOL
IF YOU GO OUT DRESSED LIKE THAT, YOU'LL BE HAULED OFF TO THE LOONY BIN!
TOTALLY LAME
LOONY BIN
NO ONE WILL BELIEVE IT
Sad
AAAAAAAAAAAAAAH!
AAAW
YIKES! WELL, AT LEAST SHE SOUNDS LIKE A SIREN!

CAZENOVE/WILLIAM

WENDY, WHATCHA DOIN'?

I HAVE TO FINISH MY MATH HOMEWORK.

THEN I GET THE COMPUTER UNTIL BEDTIME!

IN YOUR DREAMS! I'VE JUST GOT ONE POEM LEFT!

Anastasia was her name, Pretty as a picture in a frame dum da da dum da da dum tiddley-pom, tiddley-pom

GO ME! I'M DONE! THE MOUSE IS MINE!

YEAH RIGHT! I BET YOU JUST MADE UP THE ANSWERS.

WHAT ABOUT YOU? I BET YOU CAN'T RECITE A POEM.

Her name was Wendy She was ugly and unfriendly

OH, GREAT.

YEAH. NOT FAIR!

HE DIDN'T HAVE ANY HOMEWORK!

TAXES   LATE FEES

BILLS   BUDGET

CAZENOVE/WILLIAM

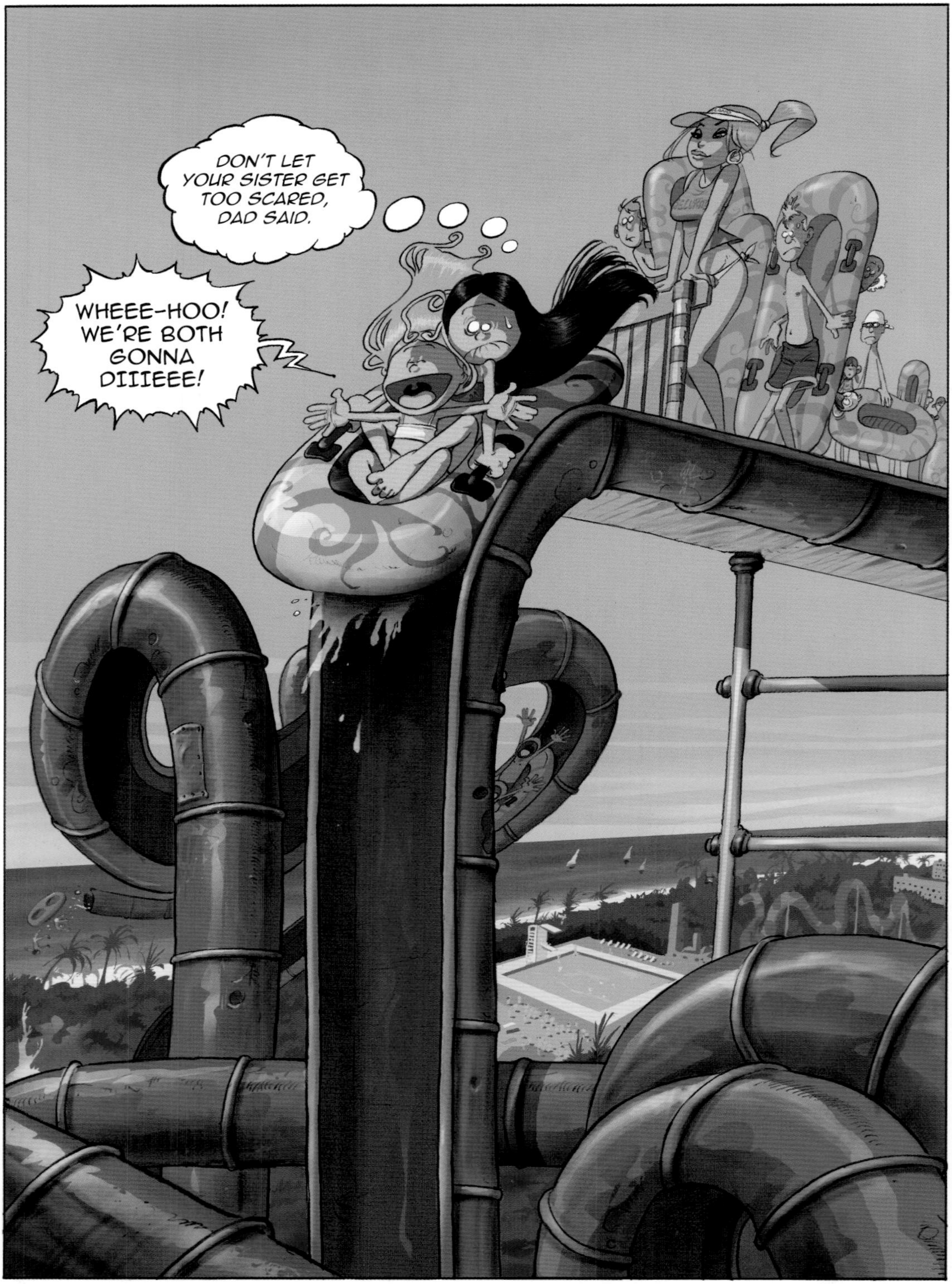
DON'T LET YOUR SISTER GET TOO SCARED, DAD SAID.
WHEEE-HOO! WE'RE BOTH GONNA DIIIEEE!
CAZENOVE/WILLIAM

LOOK AT ALL THE COSTUMES I FOUND FOR HALLOWEEN!

COOL! LET'S TRY THEM ON RIGHT NOW!

TACKY.

NOT MY CUP OF TEA.

SO LAME.

NOPE NOPE NOPE.

NOT SUBTLE.

WEIRD!

CHARMING... NOT.

CLUELESS!

Khh Khhh Khh

C'MON, SAMMIE, STOP LAUGHING AND HELP US!

LOL! YOU GIRLS CRACK ME UP.

PERSONALLY, I ALWAYS CHOOSE THE MOST RIDICULOUS COSTUME POSSIBLE... IT'S MORE FUN THAT WAY!

WOW! AWESOME-SAUCE!

YEAH! THERE'S NOTHING MORE RIDICULOUS!

CAZENOVE/WILL:AM

MY PILLOW, A DVD, CHIPS AND SWEETS...

I'M ALL SET FOR OUR SLEEPOVER!

WELL, I'M NOT!

FIRST I HAVE TO READ A BEDTIME STORY TO MAUREEN.

HOW SWEET!

AACK! I CAN'T REMEMBER WHERE I PUT HER FAVORITE BOOK!

HOW ABOUT THIS ONE?

TALES OF LITTLE QUACKIE? TOO BABYISH. SHE'S OUTGROWN IT.

THE YES YES YES BOOK?

NO NO NO!

LOOK, STORIES FROM THE BLACK CAVE.

ARE YOU NUTS? SHE'D HAVE NIGHTMARES ALL NIGHT LONG AND SPOIL OUR SLEEPOVER!

MR. PANDA ON PARADE?

NOPE.

MR. PANDA IN PEORIA?

NO WAY.

HEEY!

I FOUND IT!

SHE'LL BE OUT LIKE A LIGHT IN FIVE MINUTES.

8:30: LOCAL NEWS
9:00: "CRAZY ABOUT COOKING"
9:30: "DANCING LIFE," EPISODE 15
10:00: "ALL ABOUT CATS"
10:30: "HOW TO CLEAN YOUR ROOM"

CAZENOVE/WILLIAM

SMASH!

STOP IT THIS INSTANT, YOUNG LADIES!

CLEAN UP THIS MESS RIGHT AWAY!

HERE YA GO!!!

THEY'VE NEVER BEEN SO CLEAN!

CAZENOVE/WILLIAM

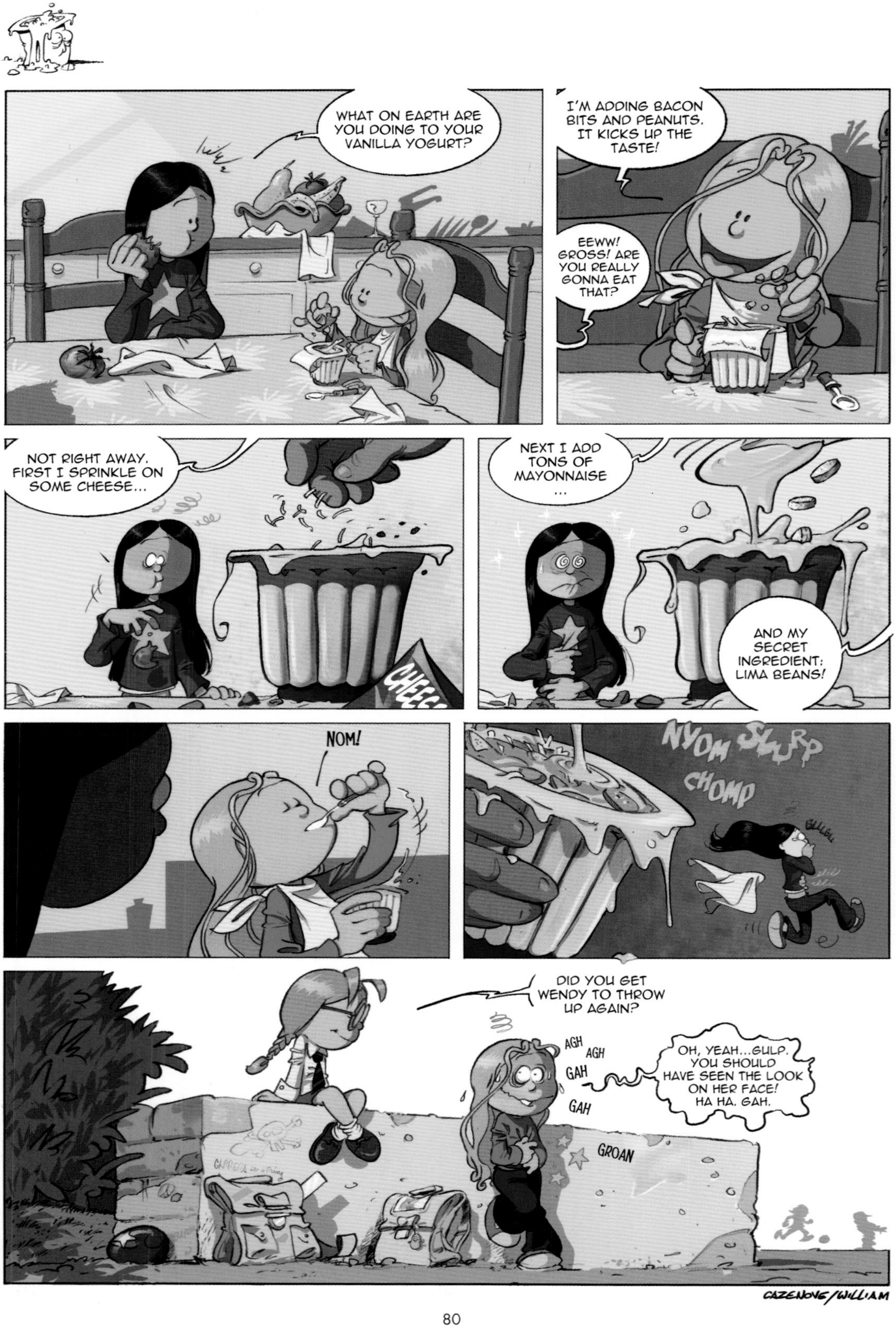
WHAT ON EARTH ARE YOU DOING TO YOUR VANILLA YOGURT?
I'M ADDING BACON BITS AND PEANUTS. IT KICKS UP THE TASTE!
EEWW! GROSS! ARE YOU REALLY GONNA EAT THAT?
NOT RIGHT AWAY. FIRST I SPRINKLE ON SOME CHEESE...
NEXT I ADD TONS OF MAYONNAISE ...
AND MY SECRET INGREDIENT: LIMA BEANS!
NOM!
NYOM SLURP
CHOMP
DID YOU GET WENDY TO THROW UP AGAIN?
AGH AGH
GAH
GAH
OH, YEAH...GULP. YOU SHOULD HAVE SEEN THE LOOK ON HER FACE! HA HA. GAH.
GROAN
CAZENOVE/WILLIAM

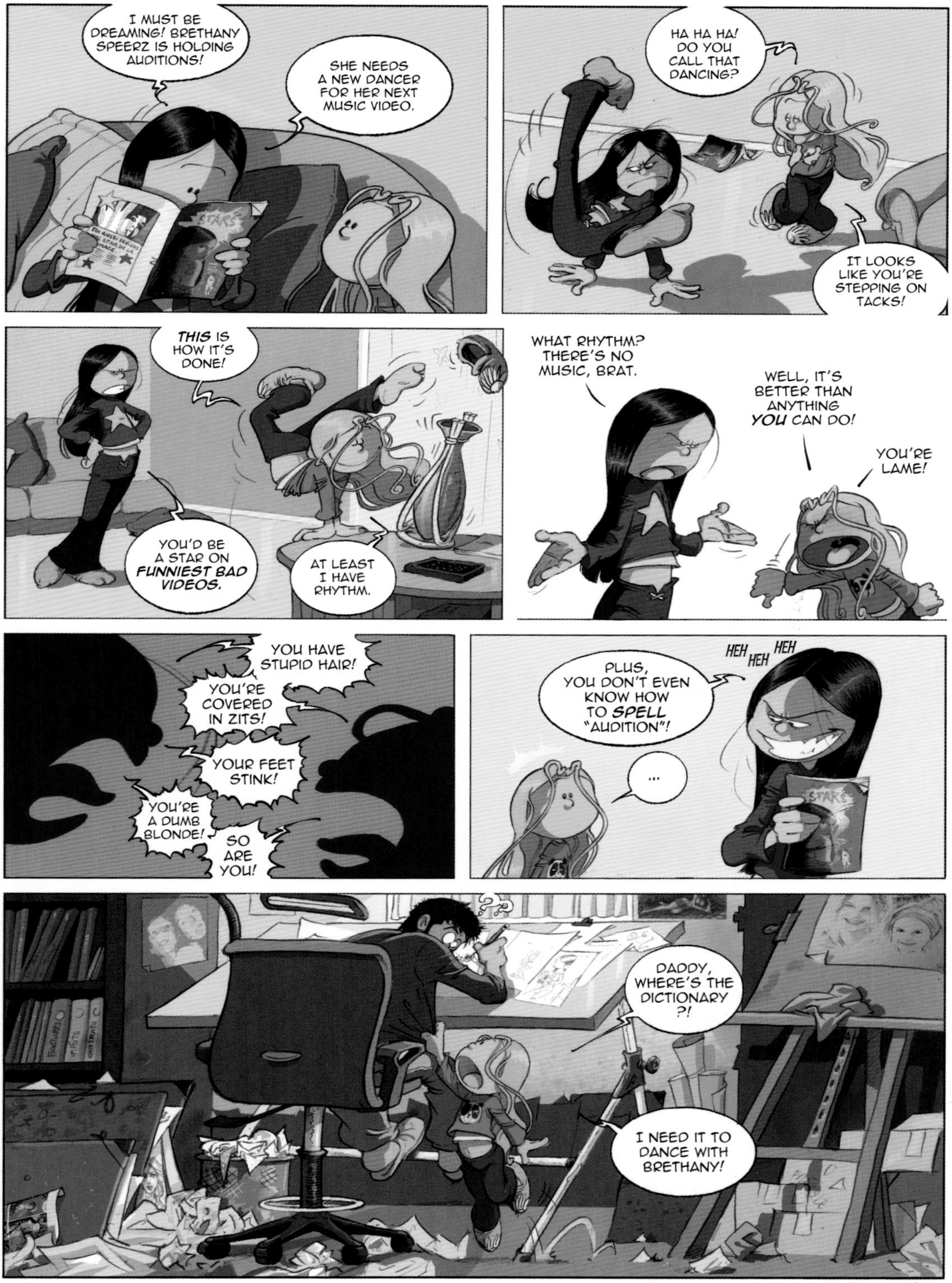
I MUST BE DREAMING! BRETHANY SPEERZ IS HOLDING AUDITIONS!
SHE NEEDS A NEW DANCER FOR HER NEXT MUSIC VIDEO.
STARS
HA HA HA! DO YOU CALL THAT DANCING?
IT LOOKS LIKE YOU'RE STEPPING ON TACKS!
THIS IS HOW IT'S DONE!
YOU'D BE A STAR ON FUNNIEST BAD VIDEOS.
AT LEAST I HAVE RHYTHM.
WHAT RHYTHM? THERE'S NO MUSIC, BRAT.
WELL, IT'S BETTER THAN ANYTHING YOU CAN DO!
YOU'RE LAME!
YOU HAVE STUPID HAIR!
YOU'RE COVERED IN ZITS!
YOUR FEET STINK!
YOU'RE A DUMB BLONDE!
SO ARE YOU!
HEH HEH HEH
PLUS, YOU DON'T EVEN KNOW HOW TO SPELL "AUDITION"!
...
STARS
DADDY, WHERE'S THE DICTIONARY ?!
I NEED IT TO DANCE WITH BRETHANY!

CAZENOVE/WILLIAM

DO YOU HAVE THE KEYS?

YEP! GET IN ON THE OTHER SIDE.

LOOK HOW HIGH I CAN BOUNCE!

THESE SEATS SURE ARE COMFY... I LIKE 'EM!

UP, DOWN, UP, DOWN...

LET'S TRY OUT THE RADIO.

I FOUND A PLACE TO PUT SODA!

THAT WOULD BE... *OVER THE TOP.*

AND IN THE BACK WE COULD PUT, LIKE, A THOUSAND VIDEO GAMES.

HOW MANY TEDDY BEARS WOULD THAT BE?

SOOOO— ARE YOU INTERESTED?

WE SHOULD HAVE ADDED ANOTHER ZERO.

THEN WE COULD BUY EVEN *MORE* CANDY!

CAZENOVE/WILL'AM

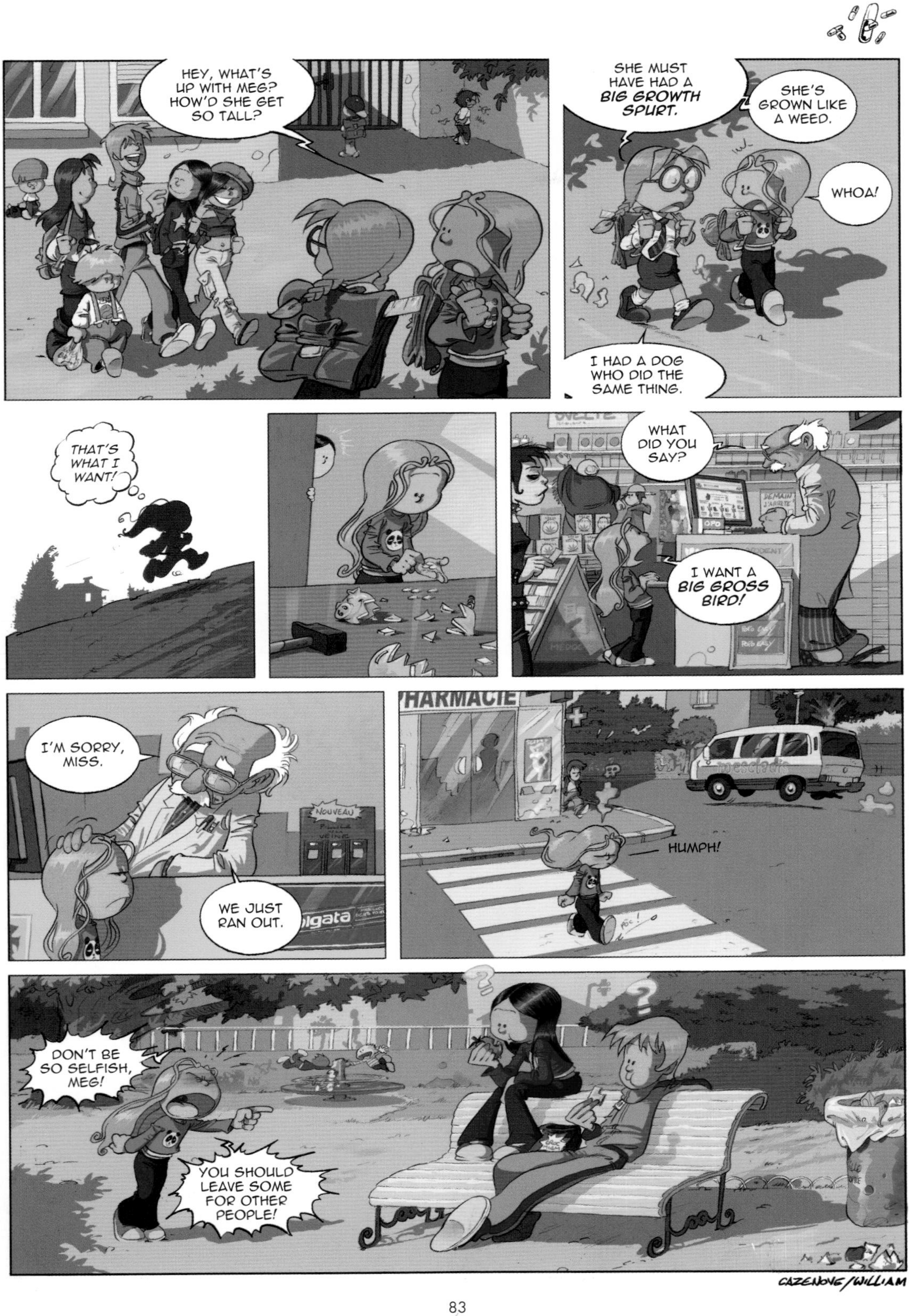
HEY, WHAT'S UP WITH MEG? HOW'D SHE GET SO TALL?
SHE MUST HAVE HAD A BIG GROWTH SPURT.
SHE'S GROWN LIKE A WEED.
WHOA!
I HAD A DOG WHO DID THE SAME THING.
THAT'S WHAT I WANT!
WHAT DID YOU SAY?
I WANT A BIG GROSS BIRD!
I'M SORRY, MISS.
WE JUST RAN OUT.
HUMPH!
DON'T BE SO SELFISH, MEG!
YOU SHOULD LEAVE SOME FOR OTHER PEOPLE!
CAZENOVE/WILLIAM

PLEASE, CAN I FLIP A PANCAKE?

YES, BUT NOT TOO HIGH, OKAY?!

HERE GOES!

SWEEEET!

NICE JOB! IT LANDED RIGHT IN THE PAN!

HOW ABOUT THAT.

YOU HAVE TO BE VERY CAREFUL WITH THE BATTER.

SPIFFY-TASTIC!

LAST ONE!

AND YOU DIDN'T EVEN SPILL A DROP ON YOUR APRON!

WE'RE SPOTLESS!

TIME TO EAT!

YES, BUT WHERE?

CAZENOVE/WILLIAM

84

RED ALERT!

RED ALERT!

SLAM!

PUBLIC HEALTH OFFICE, OUR DETECTORS HAVE PICKED UP CONTAMINATION IN THIS SECTOR.

HEY! I DIDN'T DO ANYTHING!

CONTAGION RISK LEVEL IS EXTRA...

...MEGA...

SUPER-HIGH

CONTAGE-WHAT?

STAND BACK FOR YOUR OWN SAFETY!

BEEP BEEP BEEP! I'VE DETECTED THE SOURCE OF THE INFECTION!

HELLO, BASE.

LOCKED ON TARGET!

BUT *WHO* 'FECTED *WHAT*?

YOUR BUNNY...

...IS CARRYING A VERY VERY CONTAGIOUS VIRUS...HE NEEDS IMMEDIATE DECONTAMI-NATION.

WELL PLAYED, WENDY!

I HAD NO CHOICE. IT STANK SO BAD I COULD SMELL IT FROM *MY* ROOM!

CAZENOVE/WILLIAM

WHAT ARE YOU GIVING MOM FOR HER BIRTHDAY?

THIS! I MADE A HANDPRINT IN CLAY.

YOU'RE KIDDING. THAT'S *SO* PRESCHOOL.

DFFFT!

SHE'LL LOVE IT! BESIDES, IT'S EASY TO CRITICIZE.

WHAT ARE *YOU* GONNA GET HER, BRAT?

ME? UM... I DON'T KNOW YET.

YOU'D BETTER THINK OF SOMETHING QUICK.

I'M NOT GONNA MAKE HER ANOTHER PASTA NECKLACE...

AND NOT AN ASHTRAY... SHE DOESN'T SMOKE.

WHAT WOULD BE *BETTER* THAN A CLAY HANDPRINT?

I'VE GOT IT!

THWAP!

MO-O-O-O-O-M!

HAPPY BIRTHDAY, MOM!

I'LL HAVE TO WAIT FOR IT TO DRY BEFORE I CAN WRAP IT.

CAZENOVE/WILLIAM

DON'T GET UP, DAD! I'LL MAKE COFFEE FOR YOU AND MOM.

I'LL CLEAR THE TABLE!

DON'T LIFT A FINGER!!!

JUST A QUICK TOUCH-UP WITH THE VACUUM!

NOT A SMUDGE OR FINGERPRINT ANYWHERE!

I'LL SHAKE OUT THE TABLECLOTH.

AND PLUMP UP THE CUSHIONS.

I'LL WATER THE PLANTS.

SAY, GIRLS... WHILE YOU'RE AT IT, WHY DON'T YOU CLEAN YOUR ROOMS?

?!

CLEAN OUR ROOMS? ARE YOU NUTS?

WE'VE GOT BETTER THINGS TO DO!

WHO DO YOU THINK WE ARE— YOUR MAIDS?!

CAZENOVE/WILLIAM

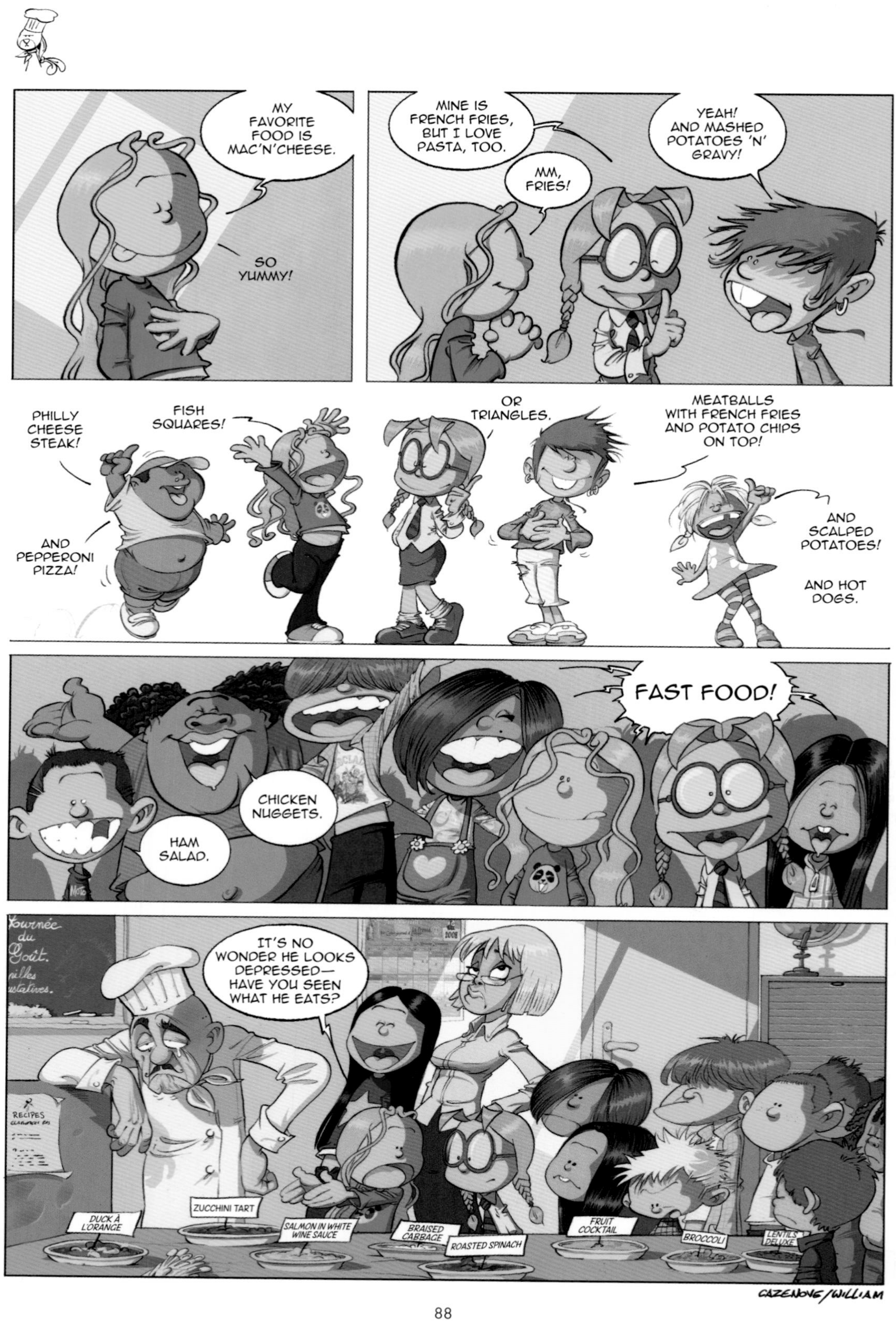
MY FAVORITE FOOD IS MAC'N'CHEESE.
SO YUMMY!
MINE IS FRENCH FRIES, BUT I LOVE PASTA, TOO.
MM, FRIES!
YEAH! AND MASHED POTATOES 'N' GRAVY!
PHILLY CHEESE STEAK!
AND PEPPERONI PIZZA!
FISH SQUARES!
OR TRIANGLES.
MEATBALLS WITH FRENCH FRIES AND POTATO CHIPS ON TOP!
AND SCALPED POTATOES!
AND HOT DOGS.
FAST FOOD!
CHICKEN NUGGETS.
HAM SALAD.
IT'S NO WONDER HE LOOKS DEPRESSED— HAVE YOU SEEN WHAT HE EATS?
RECIPES
DUCK À L'ORANGE
ZUCCHINI TART
SALMON IN WHITE WINE SAUCE
BRAISED CABBAGE
ROASTED SPINACH
FRUIT COCKTAIL
BROCCOLI
LENTILS DELUXE
CAZENOVE/WILLIAM

YEAH. I BROKE UP WITH MASON.

I HAVE TO SAY, HE GOT TO BE ANNOYING. PLUS, HE WOULDN'T STOP CHECKING OUT OTHER GIRLS.

ANYWAY— I WAS TELLING YOU ABOUT ANGELINO— SUCH A KNOCKOUT!

HE KNOCKS PEOPLE OUT?!

YEAH, IT'S TRUE HE'S EIGHTEEN. BUT HE IS SO IRRESISTIBLE!

EIGHTY ?!

THE BIG PROBLEM IS THAT HE LIVES OUT IN SPAIN...

IN OUTER SPACE ?!

TOO TRUE! IN SEVILLE... TALK ABOUT A LONG-DISTANCE RELATIONSHIP!

I CAN'T BELIEVE WENDY'S IN LOVE WITH SOMEONE SO OLD!

SHOULD I TELL OUR PARENTS OR KEEP IT TO MYSELF?

OF COURSE I'M GONNA TELL!

I SWEAR! AND HE'S AN EIGHTY-YEAR-OLD BOXING ALIEN AND HE'S NOT EVEN CIVIL TO HER!

HEY, I HAVE TO LET YOU GO, AUDREY.

I'LL FINISH TELLING YOU ABOUT THE SOAP OPERA TOMORROW!

CAZENOVE/WILLIAM

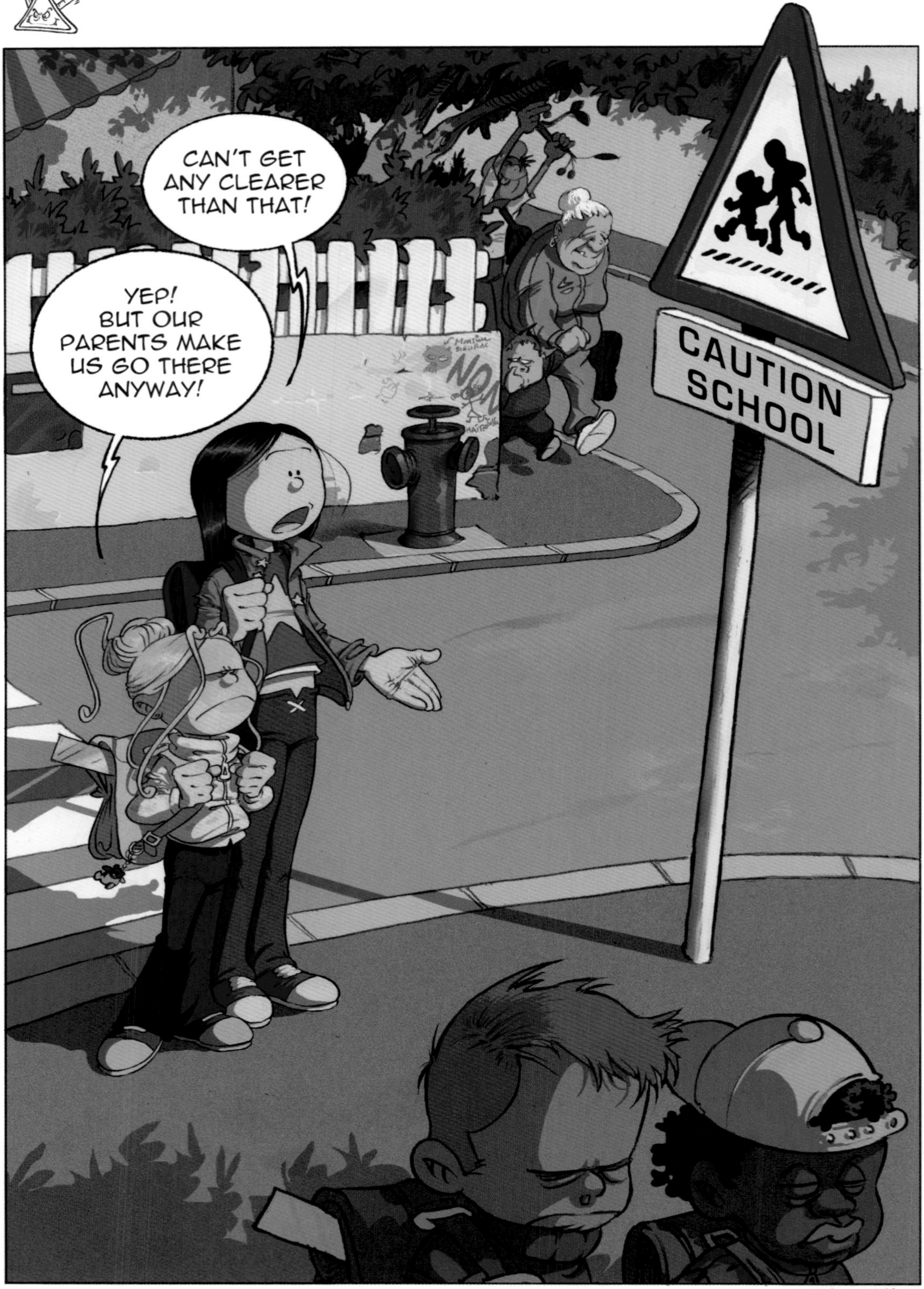

CAN'T GET ANY CLEARER THAN THAT!
YEP! BUT OUR PARENTS MAKE US GO THERE ANYWAY!
CAUTION SCHOOL

CAZENOVE/WILLIAM

NOM! SO YUMMY!

HURRY UP, MAUREEN!

JUST ONE MORE!

FINE. I'M GOING INSIDE. I DON'T WANNA CATCH A COLD.

YOU KNOW WHAT WOULD BE TOTALLY SUPER COOL, WENDY?

YEAH, SOME HOT CHOCOLATE!

BUMP!

NO—A GREAT BIG BOWL OF SNOWFLAKES...

MMM... YUMMY!

WITH RASPBERRY SYRUP ON TOP!

YOU SEE? IT'S ALWAYS THE SAME WITH YOU...

YOU ALWAYS GO OVERBOARD!

I WANNDED RASPBERRY SYRUP. NODD COUGH SYRUP.

SNIRRFFLE!

CAZENOVE/WILLIAM

91

UH-OH!
LOOK AT
THE TIME!

OH,
NO!

12:00
12:00
12:00
12:00

Ziiiip!

Zooooom!

IT CAN'T BE
TIME TO SET THE
TABLE ALREADY!

WE'D LOVE
TO HELP, BUT
OUR ARMS ARE
MEGA-FULL!

CAZENOVE/WILLIAM

WE HAVE **INDESTRUCTIBLE** COSTUMES!

SAVING THE WORLD: NO PROBLEM!

THEY STAND UP TO BULLETS...

HE, HEE! STOP TICKLING ME!

TO MISSILES...

DIDN'T EVEN HURT!

BANK!

TO NUCLEAR EXPLOSIONS ...

BOOOM

TO ROBOT DEATH RAYS ...

TO ACID-SPEWING ALIENS!

BUT THEY HAVE ONE BIG FLAW ...

...THEY DON'T STAND UP TO MATH HOMEWORK.

CAZENOVE/WILLIAM

WHEN I'M BIG, I'M GONNA BE THE BEST DOCTOR IN THE WHOLE WORLD.

DR. MAUREEN, QUICK! THERE'S AN EMERGENCY EMERGING!

I WILL ALWAYS COME AND TAKE CARE OF EVERYTHING...

MY HUSBAND CAUGHT A TERRIBLE COLD, DOCTOR...

YOU'RE HIS LAST HOPE!

NO PROBLEM! I'LL OPERATE.

WHEW!

I FEEL GREAT!

HEE HEE!

I WILL BE THE FIRST TO SUCCESSFULLY PERFORM A RIGHT-LEG TRANSPLANT.

GUESS WHAT? THE DONOR HAD TWO OF THEM...

I'LL HAVE MY OWN FAN CLUB...

WHAT BRAND OF LIPSTICK DO YOU WEAR?

WHAT WILL YOUR NEXT OPERATION BE?

ARE YOU MARRIED?

WHO MAKES YOUR CLOTHES?

WHEN DID YOU DECIDE TO BECOME A DOCTOR?

I REMEMBER THE EXACT MOMENT.

WHEN I WAS LITTLE, MY SISTER BUSTED HER LEG...

I COULDN'T BEAR TO WATCH HER SUFFER.

SO, AFTER DISCUSSING IT WITH MY BUNNY, I DECIDED TO OPERATE ON HER.

WHY ARE YOU LOOKING AT ME LIKE THAT?

CAZENOVE/WILLIAM

WATCH OUT FOR PAPERCUT

Welcome to the fight-filled first THE SISTERS graphic novel by Cazenove and William—from Papercutz, those unrelated siblings dedicated to publishing great graphic novels for all ages. I'm Jim Salicrup, the Editor-in-Chief and semi-professional Papa Smurf impersonator, and I'm here to take you behind-the-scenes at Papercutz . . .

First off, we're as proud as can be to premiere THE SISTERS, a new ongoing graphic novel series about big sister Wendy and little sister Maureen. And we're not just proud that this is a fun, smart, beautifully written and illustrated comics series, but that it's yet another series that's primarily created for girls published by Papercutz. As I just said, we're dedicated to publishing great graphic novels for all-ages, but since publisher Terry Nantier and I started Papercutz over ten years ago, we've always been proud to publish comics for girls. One our very first series was NANCY DREW Girl Detective, about the world-famous teen sleuth, who is smart, independent, and able to solve mysteries all

on her own. We think THE SISTERS continues to show our commitment to publishing great material for girls.

Now, Nancy Drew is an only child, even though her friends Bess and George are like sisters. The fact is that they're all about the same age, and that's a very different dynamic than what exists between Wendy and Maureen. In DANCE CLASS, another Papercutz graphic novel series, there's a slightly similar sisterly relationship between older sister Julie and younger sister Capucine. Because that series is focused mainly on Julie and her friends Alia and Lucie and their time together in DANCE CLASS, we don't get to see that much of Julie and Capucine's relationship. What we do see is great fun, but being sisters is not what DANCE CLASS is about, whereas THE SISTERS is all about the relationship between Wendy and Maureen.

In ERNEST & REBECCA, there have been some wonderful moments between five-and-a-half-year-old Rebecca and her much older teen sister Coralie. But Rebecca and Coralie's relationship is vastly different than Wendy and Maureen's—Coralie no longer has time for her younger sister, as she is trying to deal with all the changes in life that happen when you become a teen.

While there are even more exciting examples of siblings in other Papercutz graphic novels as well, the bigger point I'm trying to make is that it's fun to explore and see all these types of relationships in comics. All the sisters I've mentioned are different and unique, just like we all are and real life. And that's the kind of compelling subject matter that makes for the kind of fun-filled comics we're so proud to publish at Papercutz! We hope you agree—and also check out some of the other series I've mentioned. I suspect you may love them as much as we do!

Thanks,

JIM

STAY IN TOUCH!

EMAIL: salicrup@papercutz.com
WEB: www.papercutz.com
TWITTER: @papercutzgn
FACEBOOK: PAPERCUTZGRAPHICNOVELS
REGULAR MAIL: Papercutz, 160 Broadway, Suite 700, East Wing, New York, NY 10038

More fun with Wendy and Maureen coming soon in
THE SISTERS #2!

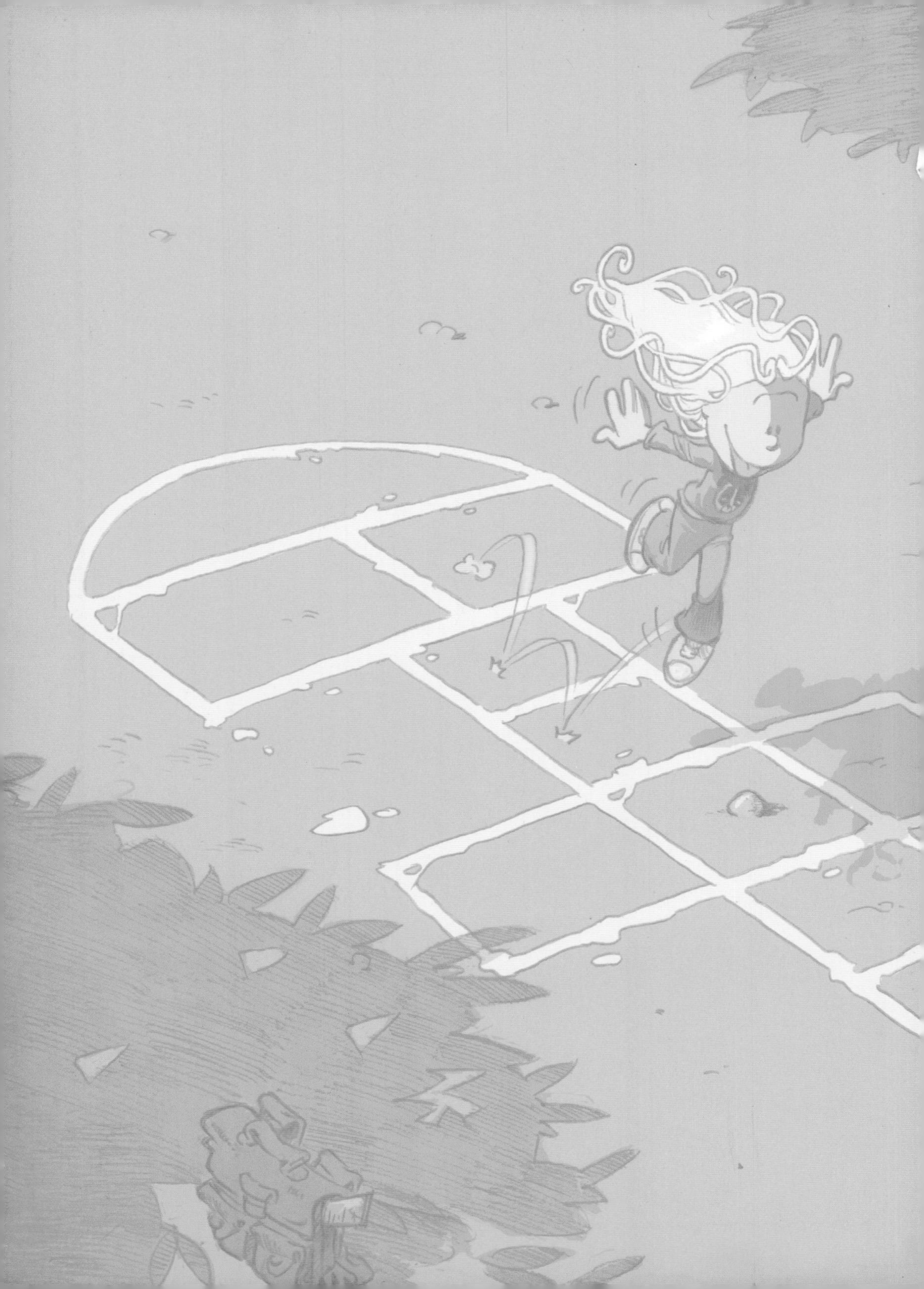